The Season for Second Chances

Ruth Saberton

Createspace Edition 2

COPYRIGHT

DEDICATION

For Kathy Wallis

A very special lady who never does anything by halves.

PROLOGUE
HALLOWS FARM DECEMBER 1968
GRACE

Grandma's house was always bitterly cold in December. It was an ancient Cornish farmhouse tucked up in the bleak folds of Bodmin Moor; it had thick granite walls, icy flagstone floors downstairs and windows that rattled when the winter storms blew in from the distant sea. Draughts puffed under the doors, lifting rugs in the chill hallways and stirring the curtains. Even the water in the washstand jugs froze. If you stayed the night you'd huddle under the blankets and shiver, with just the top of your head peeking out and your numb feet burning on a hot-water bottle. In the morning, you'd wake and see your cloudy breath before hopping across the cold lino to the window and marvelling at how Jack Frost's fingers had painted patterns on the inside of the glass while you'd been asleep.

Grace's brother, Ned, hated staying at Hallows Farm. He'd moan about the lack of heating and the outdoor toilet, and he'd have an expression Grandma described as like a "wet weekend" until it was time to go home. Now that he was fourteen, Ned didn't want to spend his holidays in Cornwall: he'd insisted on staying in the town with his friends instead.

"Don't go," he'd said this time as Grace had packed her case. "Besides, I don't know why Granny's still there. Didn't you hear what Dad said? 'That place is too big for a woman on her own and she really ought to sell it.'"

He'd said this in a perfect imitation of their father's voice, the pronunciation as crisp as the frost that had iced their neat lawn overnight. Grace had overheard the conversation too, but she'd been more struck by her mother's argument that Grandma was made of sterner stuff.

"She was a suffragette, remember?" Mummy had pointed out. "My mother was put in prison and force-fed, so I think she can cope with a farmhouse and her granddaughter."

Grace hadn't known what a suffragette was, so she'd looked it up in the big encyclopedia at school, the one that Miss Hanwell was always telling them to use, and she was even prouder of Grandma after she'd read the entry. She'd been proud of her already, of course – there was nobody who drove a Land Rover quite like Grandma or who could make plants appear so miraculously out of the mud – but when she discovered just how courageous Grandma had been, Grace thought her heart would pop. She hoped that she could be even a tiny bit as brave as that when she grew up.

The cold and the quiet of Hallows Farm didn't bother Grace. Neither did she mind how the old Land Rover rattled and coughed through the lanes when Grandma collected her from the station. Grace was just glad to be back in Cornwall. The big sky and sharp air made her spirits soar, and she was always astonished by the bleak beauty of Bodmin Moor.

This December was exceptionally bitter, but her grandmother didn't seem to notice – especially when she was in the kitchen, where the black range pumped out heat and the kettle sang merrily on the hotplate. It was in this big warm room with its huge fireplace blackened by centuries of soot and its dresser crammed with preserves and pickles that Grace loved to spend time with Grandma. Here they would cook stews, bake cakes and bottle rich damson gin made from the fruit collected out of the hedgerows. As her grandmother worked, her deft hands slicing or kneading, Grace would stand on a stool and watch in amazement. Seeing the ingredients coming together was like magic, especially when one of her grandmother's concoctions began bubbling away in the cauldron above the fire.

But this weekend was extra special. It was the first Sunday in December: time to make the mincemeat for Grandma's delicious mince pies, cakes and plum puddings.

"It's time I passed my secret recipe on to you," she told Grace solemnly. "Are you watching carefully?"

Her grandmother's eyes were as bright and beady as the piles of currants waiting to be mixed with the ringlets of orange peel and bone-white suet.

Grace nodded. "Yes, Grandma."

"So make sure you listen up. We can't have the secret dying with me, can we? Not that I'm going anywhere for years – but when I do, it's going to be your job to make the mincemeat and take care of all the Christmas traditions. There's the tree and the decorations and sharing the food with friends and making sure the house is loved. Do you think you can do all that?"

"Yes," Grace answered. None of this seemed hard. She adored Christmas and she especially liked Grandma's Christmas baking. Just the thought of the mince pies and plum puddings made her mouth water.

"Good," said Grandma. "Then it's time for you to learn my secret recipe. We want the mincemeat to be moist and delicious so that our friends and loved ones enjoy every mouthful. Making food with love is the secret. That's the ingredient only *you* can add."

Grace's eyes were wide. "But how do you do that?"

Her grandmother smiled. "By thinking happy thoughts, sending everyone your love and stirring in blessings, of course. Now, tip the fruit into the dish.'

"All of it?"

"All of it. Don't hold back."

Together they tipped the fruit into an enormous cream mixing bowl. Blushing cranberries, glossy cherries as red as Mummy's lipstick, wizened sultanas and raisins, plump prunes and little dots of currants all tumbled together to form a jewel-bright mix of fruits. As she helped tilt the bowl, Grace thought hard about all the people she loved the most and wished them all the good things she could think of. How this part of the recipe worked she wasn't sure. Maybe her benevolence drifted into the bowl? Or perhaps the fruit sucked it up like orange squash up a straw? The spell was certainly effective though, because Grandma's cakes and mince pies always tasted wonderful.

"And now for the other secret ingredients," said Grandma. Crossing the kitchen, she reached onto her tiptoes for two bottles that had spent the whole year slumbering on the top shelf of the dresser. "Brandy and rum. Now, half a bottle of each is the usual recipe but I'm never one to do things in half measures and I don't think you are either, Grace, so a whole bottle of each. There's no point being half-hearted."

Her grandmother unscrewed the cap of the brandy bottle and instantly the kitchen was filled with the smell of Christmas.

"And that's the most important secret ingredient," Grace's grandmother told her as they sloshed the amber liquid over the glossy fruit. "And I'm not referring to the alcohol, mind you. The secret to everything – whether it's baking a cake or living a good life – is never to be half-hearted. Never do things in half measures, Grace. When you do something, give it your all: pour your heart and soul in. Follow your passion. No half measures. In life, love and friendship. You won't forget that, will you? Even when it feels like an impossible thing to do."

Grace shook her head. "I won't forget, Grandma."

When you were eight nothing seemed impossible, especially at Christmas when the world was full of magic and the frosty landscape outside glittered like the Snow Queen's crown. Grace was sure she would never, ever forget her grandmother's secret ingredient.

Grace Anders would never do anything by halves.

CHAPTER 1
PRESENT DAY
GRACE

The drive to Cornwall was agonisingly slow. Traffic crawled around the M25, limped along the M4 and juddered down the M5 in leg-aching fits and starts. Tail lights dotted the Blackdown Hills like festive red beads. On the opposite carriageway, a corresponding line of headlamps stretched into the distance; they reminded Grace of white fairy lights, like the ones she always wound through the garlands atop the mantelpieces at Hallows Farm.

As the traffic queued, Grace ran through her mental checklist of all the jobs she had to do on arrival. Even as she'd locked the door of her flat and stepped into the 4 a.m. darkness, she'd already been miles away from London and settling into her Cornish house. As far as Grace was concerned, Christmas only began when she turned the heavy brass key in the farmhouse door and stepped over the threshold. Once her feet were treading the worn flagstones and the kettle was set to boil on the Aga hotplate, she could exhale deeply and feel the weight of everyday life tumbling away.

And it was a weight, Grace reflected, although one she had willingly shouldered. For most of the year she was flat out in her role as general secretary of one of Britain's biggest trade unions. Busy didn't even come close: she barely had time to breathe.

Grace loved every minute of her work and considered it an honour to have been voted into the position. Accordingly, she gave her job her all. Her grandmother's advice might have been uttered a long time ago but Grace had never forgotten it; she had taken the words to heart and had lived them – which was probably why she was absolutely shattered.

Maybe it was time to look at the future and have a rethink, though? Perhaps she should consider standing down, instead of putting herself forward for re-election. This idea terrified her, but lately she'd felt more and more certain that the time had come to make some changes. Big changes.

It was rare that Grace managed to have a break from things, so she was looking forward to escaping to Hallows Farm again. Ever since her grandmother had left it to Grace in her will (a decision that had amazed and incensed various members of her family in equal measure), she had spent what little spare time she had there. In particular, it had become her tradition to spend the festive season in Cornwall: no matter how hectic her schedule or heavy her workload, she would return to visit the farm. Each year, she'd festoon the house with greenery and weave fairy lights through the banisters, before decorating the Christmas tree that the next-door farmer always delivered. Grace loved to bake, and within hours of her arrival there would be mince pies cooking in the Aga and mulled wine simmering on the hotplate. Anyone who dropped by was always sure of a warm welcome. Over the years it had become a custom for friends and neighbours to pop in during Christmas Eve. Grace liked to think this was to see her, but she suspected that the treats made using her grandmother's recipes were the real reason.

As her journey wound westward, the lanes grew narrower and the landscape shifted from wooded valleys and gently sloping pastures to sparse moorland and bleak outcrops of granite. Shaggy ponies clipped the grass and small grey villages clustered around stubby churches and listing gravestones. With every mile that brought her closer to Hallows Farm, Grace's heart rose. This was her home, in a way that the city flat never could be; here there was a sense of belonging that she never found in London. Her brother Ned would be sulking at home, and her poor niece, Poppy, probably wouldn't be speaking to anyone unless she had to. Grace might not have a husband or children of her own to share Hallows with, but there were friends here who felt just like family.

This was enough, Grace told herself. It had to be. She couldn't ask for, or expect, more now. How could she? It was way too late for all that now. Alas, one thing her grandmother hadn't explained was that sometimes *not doing things by halves* came at a high price. Grace sighed as she turned onto the bumpy lane that led to the village of Higher Hallows. There would be plenty of opportunities to pore over her bittersweet memories on Boxing Day, when her guests had departed and the silence became so heavy it was almost a noise. Right now, it was Christmas and she was nearly home.

It was already mid-morning and Grace had been driving since

before dawn. She could hardly wait to stop. With any luck John Tuckett, the elderly farmer next door, would have delivered the logs, lit the fire and placed the tree in the sitting room. These were all jobs he'd been doing for her every year, for as long as she could remember.

The lane twisted sharply to the left, then dropped into a valley – and there was Hallows at last! A medieval longhouse that looked as much a part of the landscape as though it had grown from the Cornish soil, it was set back from the road and surrounded by a large garden, which was all that remained of the original farm. Grace's grandmother had eventually admitted defeat when it had come to working the land, so most of it had been sold off to the Tucketts – including a couple of cottages that were now let as holiday homes, having been smartened up with fresh white paint and sage woodwork. Grace noticed that the lights were off in both and that a shiny black Jeep was parked outside John's farmhouse. She was intrigued. Usually her neighbour favoured his Defender, an ancient vehicle mostly held together by dog hair and mud. Did John have visitors? This seemed unlikely, given that the grumpy old farmer made Heathcliff look sociable. Even his own family gave him a wide berth, especially since Mark—

Grace pulled her thoughts up short, laughing despairingly at herself for still feeling a pang almost forty years on. How ridiculous! She wasn't a teenager and neither was Mark Tuckett. He was more or less the same age as her and was now a man in his late fifties, with a grown family and an entire life she knew nothing about. The boy she'd loved was long gone, lost in the past along with the girl she used to be. What could have been was buried there too, and it was best that way. For Grace her first love was forever eighteen, with a full head of glossy black curls, laughing green eyes and cinnamon sprinkles on the bridge of his nose. His arms were as strong as ever, and just the memory of his slow smile was still enough to make her heart leap into her throat. She'd never had to witness him age or bald or grow stooped or marry somebody else. He'd been her first kiss and somebody else would be his last, but Mark Tuckett lived in her heart just as vividly and vibrantly as the day they'd said goodbye.

Mark had longed to travel and see the world. The thought of Australia had made his eyes shine, and he'd wanted Grace to come with him. But how could she? Her future had been mapped out. A levels. University. Changing the world. No half measures. It was all or nothing – and if she sometimes lay awake wondering if she'd made the right choices, then maybe this was the sacrifice she'd had to make.

This wasn't the time to be melancholy, she told herself sharply. It was Christmas and she was home. This was a time to celebrate, relax and be with people she cared about. Regrets and reminiscences could wait until New Year's Eve. Besides, from what little Grace had gleaned about Mark over the years, he'd done just fine. More than fine. The last she'd heard, he was a surgeon in Cairns. He'd come a long way from being a farmer's son with a head full of dreams, that was for sure. She'd probably done him a favour in the long run.

Cheered by this thought, Grace parked alongside the house and killed the engine. Her fingers were stiff from gripping the wheel for over five hours and she flexed them slowly, wincing as the blood tingled them awake. She could hardly wait to get inside, put the kettle on and sit down with a cup of tea. Then, when she felt more human, she'd fetch her bags from the boot and think about warming the mince pies. Perhaps she could even make a start on the tree before her visitors arrived.

Outside the warm fug of her car, the sharp air came as a shock. Cornwall was gripped in winter's fierce embrace; the grass was still stiff with frost, and spiders' webs laced the hedges. Grace's breath made flowers in the air and her nose stung with cold. The sky was plump with clouds, bruise yellow and brooding with the threat of bad weather. She frowned. Surely it wasn't going to snow? It rarely snowed in Cornwall.

I should have checked the forecast, Grace thought as she slipped her hand under the doormat to search for the key. Then again, did it really matter if she was snowed in for a day or two? It wasn't as though there was somewhere she was meant to be or people who were expecting her to visit them. She had enough food to last a week and John would have chopped sufficient wood to keep the Aga going and the wood burner fed. It wasn't going to be like her grandmother's time, when the house had always seemed colder indoors than it was outside. The new radiators she'd installed a few years ago had seen to that, as had thick feather duvets and a toasty electric blanket.

Oh! This was very odd. Where was the key? Grace's fingers

scrabbled under the bristly mat but, rather than brushing the cool brass, they met dry leaves and something scuttling (which might or might not be a beetle). Exasperated, she bent down even lower, wincing at the way her knees ached these days, and flipped the heavy mat aside.

The key wasn't there.

Just great. This was not what she needed after a long drive and with several bags of shopping defrosting in the boot. John was getting forgetful; every time Grace called he was harder to talk to, and he hadn't even picked up last night when she'd phoned to remind him of her visit. This had alarmed Grace. Usually he'd grumble and say he didn't need reminding, given that she arrived on Christmas Eve every year just like bloody Santa – but it was unlike him not to answer at all. John was in his eighties now and, as much as he might deny it, he looked frailer each time she saw him. He refused to have any dealings with mobile phones and spurned the Internet too. Concerned about her elderly neighbour, Grace had called her friend Isolde, who lived further along, but she'd not answered either. She was probably on a ramble to the remotest part of the moors to sketch the standing stones or photograph something, Grace had thought. There'd been little choice but to hope for the best.

The trouble was, Grace wasn't just anxious about John now but worried about Isolde too. Her friend had lost her husband only a few months before and Grace knew she missed him dreadfully. Walnut-skinned, twinkle-eyed Alan and silver-haired Isolde had been the best-suited couple Grace had ever known. They'd both been teachers prior to retiring to their beloved Cornwall. Isolde had taught art and Alan had specialised in photography. All the passion they'd once given to their jobs had been poured into restoring their old engine house, working in the community shop and researching local history, although they'd continued to paint and photograph as well. Grace had spent many fascinating evenings sitting at their kitchen table drinking Alan's potent elderberry wine, and she'd counted them as two of her dearest friends. To see Alan fade away and know that she'd never again hear his infectious bark of a laugh – "like a fat, boozy seal" was how Isolde fondly described it – was painful beyond belief. Grace could only imagine how hard the loss must be for his wife.

Cancer was so cruel.

She shook her head, wanting to shake these thoughts away. It was Christmas Eve and a time to be cheerful. Isolde was bound to be out walking the dogs and she'd be here soon enough for mulled wine and tree decorating. If her friend could be brave at this emotive time of year, then Grace could certainly do her best not to crumple when they talked about Alan. They would have a lovely time. Farmer John was bound to stay for a bit too. There might also be some unexpected guests, since Grace always sent pretty cards to the holiday cottages along the road, inviting their occupants in for mulled wine. It was always pot luck whether any holidaymakers turned up and what sort of folk they were, but Grace liked people to feel wanted at Hallows, even if they were only visiting for a short time. It was her tradition.

Or it would be if she could only get into her house.

Grace wiggled the door handle in frustration and, to her surprise, the door swung open. Oh! John must have forgotten to lock up and replace the key. He'd definitely been inside to light the Aga though; as she stepped inside, the warmth wrapped around her like a hug. The radiators were belting out heat and when she rested her hand on the cream flank of the Aga it was toasty. A fully stacked basket of logs rested beside it and, glancing into the garden, Grace was pleased to see that the wood store was full. Now let the weather do its worst!

She unwound her scarf and was just reaching for the kettle when the sound of chair legs scraping flagstones made her start. Unlike Isolde, who was all in favour of blaming everything on spirits, Grace knew the sound of her grandmother's heavy furniture being dragged about when she heard it. Her heart skittered. Somebody was in the sitting room.

Then she laughed. Of course! It must be John. That was why the door wasn't locked. He hadn't forgotten at all; he was still inside and setting up the tree. Still smiling at herself for being so easily unnerved, she placed the kettle back on the hotplate and wandered along the corridor to the sitting room. This part of the house, with its cavernous fireplace and plump sofas, was where she always hung the Christmas greenery and placed the tree John selected for her. Sure enough, there he was, balancing on a chair at the far end of the room and draping white lights across the boughs.

Grace frowned. This was odd. John never put her lights up. Usually it was as much as he could do to fix the tree stand – and he only did that because he didn't trust a woman to do it properly. He never clambered onto chairs and neither was he six feet tall, or broad shouldered, or blessed with a shaggy mop of midnight curls…

Recognition broke over Grace like a wave and, as her head whirled, she clutched the edge of the table for support.

This wasn't John Tuckett. It was his son, Mark.

CHAPTER 2
NICK

Nick York was having a very strange Christmas Eve.

At lunchtime things had been looking quite ordinary. Nick had finished work early and declined the offer of drinks with his senior colleagues in favour of heading straight home. As he was rarely ever back before seven, his early return would be a big surprise for Lisa. Not only that, but they could begin the long journey to the West Country cottage they were renting long before the rest of London began its Yuletide exodus. Nick was pleased by this idea, since crawling along the M25 in peak traffic wouldn't have been the best start to a relaxing Christmas break.

A break from work. Thank God. Nick could hardly wait. The thought of not being buried in case notes and legal documents for at least a few days made Nick very happy. Maybe he'd even get time to take his camera out on the moors. Cornwall's scoured light and craggy granite tors would be wonderful to photograph. Photography was his passion, and only his father's disapproval at the mention of an arts-based degree had stopped Nick pursuing it as a career. If arguing with Edward York QC was difficult for top barristers, then it had been practically impossible for his eighteen-year-old son – so off Nick had dutifully gone to study law. In any case, his father was probably right: there was more money to be made in the legal profession than as a jobbing photographer and, yes, he probably would have been useless. Still, it might have been nice to find out. Whenever he had a spare moment, out came his camera and he would become utterly absorbed in capturing unusual angles and subtle changes in light.

As he'd left the office that afternoon, his colleagues had already been pulling on their coats and heading to the latest wine bar of choice. Carols had been playing in the lobby and the girls manning reception had been happily getting stuck into the Quality Streets. Nick had smiled as he'd bowled through the revolving door and pinged out into the sharp December cold. It had to be Christmas because usually everyone had his or her nose firmly pressed to the grindstone. There was barely time to draw breath, never mind party.

Lawrence and Coombes was one of the most prestigious law firms in the City and they asked a lot of their staff. The hours were long and they didn't end when Nick arrived home either; it wasn't unusual for him to find himself preparing for the next day well into the small hours before snatching a few hours' sleep and rising early to do it all over again. If he sometimes felt a bit like a hamster on a wheel, he'd remind himself sharply that it was a very lucrative wheel and one that paid the mortgage on the pretty mews house Lisa was adamant they had to have. And if he also found himself wishing he could step away from the pressure and be a photographer instead, then Nick had to stamp on the thought very hard. *That* was just a dream. It wasn't real life.

Nick was planning to wind down for the festive period, but this wouldn't happen at the firm's party or in a wine bar or even working his way through some chocolates while watching a film. This Christmas he'd arranged something special: he was going to surprise Lisa by whisking her away to Cornwall. Things had felt strained between them lately and Lisa had been quiet and distant. Maybe he was neglecting her by working such long hours, Nick reflected, but what choice did he have? After all, the lifestyle they enjoyed – or maybe he should more accurately say the lifestyle she enjoyed – didn't come cheap. Occasionally he questioned whether it was all worth it, but everyone had doubts at some point, didn't they? Wondering whether you were making the right choices wasn't that unusual. Look at all those guys in their forties who suddenly bought sports cars and started dating nineteen-year-old blondes.

Hold on. He was still under thirty, just about. Wasn't he a little young for a mid-life crisis? The idea of spending the next forty years of his life feeling like this was appalling.

These were the thoughts that had been whirling around Nick's mind as he'd sat on the Underground train and counted down the stations until his stop. He was simply burnt out from work, he'd decided as the stations had passed in a blur of posters and darkness; that was why he was feeling low. A week in Cornwall was just what he needed to recharge his batteries. He and Lisa could spend time together, walk in the fresh air, eat comfort food in cosy country pubs and curl up in the evenings in front of a roaring log fire. They'd have fun again, make plans (maybe even love?) and hopefully his insides would stop knotting with a strange unease he couldn't name.

With every rumble of the train's wheels Nick had felt more and more optimistic. It was hard not to when his fellow passengers were smiling and excited. Although in true Londoner style nobody broke the unwritten *don't speak on the Underground* rule, the air of anticipation was palpable. When Lisa saw the quaint cottage he'd chosen for their Christmas escape, Nick was sure that she'd be thrilled – even if being miles from the city didn't usually fill her with enthusiasm. With its white rippled walls, sage windows and gleaming wooden floorboards strewn with colourful rugs, the cottage was the perfect choice for a cosy winter getaway. She could forget hobbling around in those uncomfortable heels of hers and slip into her Uggs, leave her make-up off and give her hair a rest from the straighteners for a while.

If she wanted to, that was.

The walk home from the station only took five minutes. As he followed the familiar route past smart townhouses and flats, each glossy door festooned with a Christmas garland and each bay window twinkling with white lights artfully arranged on an expensive non-drop tree, Nick thought back to when he'd first met Lisa. Three years ago at the wedding of a family friend he'd been unable to take his eyes off the slim, blonde and impossibly elegant bridesmaid. When she'd agreed to meet him for a drink Nick had felt as though he'd won the lottery – and, amazingly, she'd seemed to feel the same way about him.

Lisa worked in PR and was scarily ambitious. Together they were the ultimate young and successful couple with high-flying careers, a house in a smart neighbourhood and a brand-new Range Rover parked outside. In fairness to his girlfriend, Nick had genuinely thought he was ambitious too. He'd certainly tried to be and on paper he was making all the right moves. Recently, though, he'd found himself daydreaming about escaping the rat race and living a simpler life.

Unfortunately, and to use one of Lisa's favourite expressions, *that wasn't going to happen*. She already had her heart set on moving to Kensington and this wouldn't come cheap. Neither would the private schools and nannies and tennis coaches that the next twenty years or so required. Nick felt his heart race at the thought. He had to talk to her. He had to. The life she was planning for them, with a thoroughness that was quite terrifying, wasn't the life he wanted. Nick was hoping that a break in Cornwall would help Lisa see there could be something different for them. Something more.

He put his key in the lock and then froze. He wasn't sure how he knew, some atavistic sixth sense maybe, but instantly Nick was aware that the house wasn't empty. The place felt different somehow, the air vibrated with an alien energy and, as he stepped into the hallway and caught sight of a leather biker jacket slung over the banisters and a pair of Timberlands kicked off by the bottom stair, Nick knew straight away what was going on. Perhaps he'd always known deep down. Lisa had been distant for months. He'd told himself that it was because she was tired from work or that she was fed up with him putting in such long hours, but now it all made sense. This wasn't about work or him or even her. It was about their relationship being over. If he was honest, it had been for some time.

As though in a dream, Nick found himself following the groaning and gasping that came from the bedroom. His hand hovered over the door handle before he turned away and headed back downstairs again. He didn't need or want to see this. It answered so many questions and suddenly he felt as though he was stepping out of the fog and into bright sunshine.

He'd been such an idiot. How many times had he given up his plans because they weren't what Lisa wanted? Or felt trapped in a life that was gradually rubbing his soul raw, like an outgrown shoe exacerbating a blister? He'd thought that relationships were about compromising and putting the other person first, but he'd forgotten that in doing this he was making himself miserable and cheating them both. He wasn't being honest with Lisa and she certainly wasn't being honest with him. He might not have betrayed her physically, but maybe holding back the truth from her was just a different type of deception.

How much of their relationship was based on falsehoods?

Nick was hurt, of course he was, and he was angry that she couldn't have just told him their relationship was over rather than letting him find out like this. And yet, at that moment, he knew for certain that he didn't love Lisa. If he did, he would have stormed into the bedroom, punched the other guy's lights out and fought for her. Instead, all he could think about was getting away. He retrieved his camera from the sitting-room cupboard but, as he looked around their home, he couldn't think of anything else he wanted to take. The whole place was Lisa's taste. Modern. Minimal. Painfully chic. His not being there wouldn't change a thing.

Maybe Nick wasn't thinking straight – or rather, he was now *finally* thinking straight – but he grabbed the car keys from the hall table. It was time to leave. Clothes and material goods he could buy; time and self-respect he couldn't. He had to get away as fast as possible but his hands were shaking so much that the keys slithered from his grasp and fell onto the parquet floor with a clatter.

"Nick?"

Lisa was standing at the top of the stairs, hastily gathering her white bathrobe around her. Her face was pale and her blue eyes were wide.

"What are you doing home at lunchtime, babe?"

"Not the same as you," Nick said. He searched his heart for the pain that should be there but he couldn't find it. He had done his grieving for this relationship a long time ago. He bent down to scoop up the fallen keys. He couldn't wait to get outside. The heat belting out from the radiators and the cloying scent of Christmas air freshener were choking him.

Lisa pulled the bathrobe tighter across her chest. "We need to talk."

It was a bit late in the day for that, Nick thought wryly.

"I don't think there's much to say, is there? You're seeing somebody else. He's here now, probably hiding in the wardrobe like a character from a bad sitcom, isn't he? That makes talking a little awkward."

She had the good grace to look ashamed. "I didn't mean… I didn't want it to be like this."

Nick opened the front door and smiled sadly up at her, the beautiful girl he'd once thought he'd loved and whom he'd tried so hard to please. Suddenly he wondered why. Love wasn't about sacrificing yourself. It was about being with someone who made you the best person you could be, who opened the cage door and wanted you to spread your wings and fly.

"Happy Christmas, Lisa," he said, and stepped into the cold afternoon to discover where his flight from the cage would take him.

CHAPTER 3
MARK

As he shifted his weight on the hard chair, Mark Tuckett reflected on how he hadn't anticipated spending Christmas in England. Since he'd left his homeland, almost forty years ago now, the festive season had come to mean sunny days spent on the beach, a dip in the ocean and a game of softball, followed by a barbie by the pool. These were all Aussie clichés, of course, but nonetheless ones he enjoyed. His home – or maybe he should say his ex-home, since Chrissie had kept it as part of the settlement – was filled with framed snapshots of Em and Rob wearing Santa hats and opening presents in the sun-drenched yard or splashing in the surf. Christmas in Cairns was about as far removed from its English counterpart as the weather.

Had it always been this cold in Cornwall? Mark couldn't really remember. He was probably used to it back then. Big sweaters, thick socks, scarves and heavy coats had been as much a part of daily life as feeding the animals or driving the tractor. The farmhouse had been warmer then though; he was sure of that. On his unexpected return last week, Mark had been shocked at just how chilly it was inside the building. As he'd tentatively explored his old home, the layers of the present peeling away to reveal the place he remembered, his heart had broken to see how his father was now living.

Without his wife to look after him, John Tuckett had taken to camping out in the kitchen. When Mark had peeped inside the sitting room, the place smelt musty, of things too long kept shut, and he'd closed the door again quickly. There was no heating apart from a fan heater in the kitchen that coughed out dusty puffs of air; the old range hadn't been lit for a long time. Apart from a packet of curling bacon, a rubbery heel of cheese and some milk with a suspicious odour, the fridge had been bare. The bread bin had been full of mouldering loaves.

It was clear that his father wasn't coping. Further exploration had revealed a cupboard crammed with pills. Moreover, judging from the thick dust on the stairs and the blankets heaped on the chair in the kitchen, his father was no longer sleeping upstairs. The only surprising thing was that he hadn't fallen sooner.

How on earth had he been running the farm?

By sheer willpower, Mark thought as he sat beside the hospital bed and watched his father sleep. There was no other explanation. John Tuckett was a determined man. Set in his ways (or bloody stubborn, more like), he'd sooner die in the attempt than ask for help – and if he'd fallen at the house rather than in the village he'd probably have had his wish.

His father shifted in the hospital bed and Mark's heart twisted with pity and love. John was in a side room off the main ward and dozing at last, even though the blind was raised and the daylight was streaming in. Outside, the sky swelled with cloud and the light was turning the strange yellowy hue that Mark remembered used to promise snow and, with it, the fun of sledging and days off school. To think that this frail figure in the bed, drowsy from medication and exhausted after the operation to set his hip, had once towed him and his sister on their sledge and hurled snowballs at them… It seemed impossible today. Impossible and heartbreaking.

How had he failed to realise just how old and weary John had become?

Because you stayed away too long, Mark told himself bluntly. He'd allowed years of resentment and hurt to keep him on the other side of the world, apart from a few brief visits. Anger at his father for not encouraging his dream of being a doctor, fear that if he stayed those dreams would slip away and, most of all, the pain of Grace's rejection—

His breath caught. Ridiculous that even after so long it still hurt so much. Maybe that was how it was with first love? Didn't they say the first cut was the deepest? He and Grace had been teenagers, little more than kids, and what they'd had wasn't real – even if it had felt more real than anything he'd known before or since. If Mark was honest with himself, it wasn't his father who'd driven him away so much as Grace's decision to go to Oxford rather than travel with him. If there had been a chance, even a slim one, that she'd have waited for him, would he have come back?

The clawing sensation in his chest was all the answer Mark needed. How was it that he could fix other people's hearts but not his own?

There was a festive air in the ward. The lunch trolley was being trundled along by two women wearing tinsel and flashing badges, and the nurses' station was overflowing with chocolates and sweets donated by grateful patients and families. Mark had worked enough Christmas shifts to appreciate how hard the staff tried to make everyone feel cheerful. It wasn't their fault it wasn't working for him. His marriage had ended. His children had grown up. His father was in hospital with a broken hip and the future of the family farm hanging in the balance.

It didn't feel like a particularly happy Christmas.

Logically, Mark knew his father's fall wasn't his fault, even if it felt like it. John Tuckett wasn't inclined to make any concessions to twenty-first century living and, unable to Skype or FaceTime his father, Mark had had to make do with a weekly telephone call. When she'd been alive, his mum had been the one to do the chatting. Elsie Tuckett had passed away ten years ago though, and Mark's father was a man of few words. Each week Mark learned that the farm was fine, his father was fine and that everything else was (no surprises for guessing the answer) also fine. Mark had suspected this wasn't quite true. His father was getting old, and working the land was becoming an issue. When Mark had last visited Cornwall three years ago, he'd tried his best to persuade John that maybe the time had come to take a step back and sell up. At this suggestion, his father had been horrified and furious in equal measure. Harsh words had been spoken, leaving Mark in no doubt that his father saw his medical career and Antipodean life as a downright betrayal. The subject hadn't been broached since.

I should have said something. I should have come over sooner.

Mark stared miserably down at the floor. Life had sped ahead in the way that it always did. His job was demanding and then the divorce had taken what was left of his energy. He'd assumed John was fine.

Well, he'd take a sabbatical and get more involved in things now, Mark promised silently. He'd let out his recently purchased house in Australia and do what he could to help his father. John wasn't going to be returning to the farm for a while, if at all, and there was certainly no way he would ever run the place again. What was going to happen next was anyone's guess and Mark's head ached from trying to think about it all.

The phone call had come out of the blue. It had been early evening and Mark had been relaxing on the deck of his new home, a cold beer in one hand and a book in the other, looking forward to kicking back after a busy day. It had been one hell of a year and to be settled at last in this small house with its hillside views and lack of history gave him a great sense of pleasure. His work was stressful and, in the past, returning home to his wife had been even more so. The silences, the back turned on him in bed and the heavy sighs had meant that working extra shifts and covering for colleagues had become more and more attractive. Even though Mark had guessed that these long hours only added to his marital problems, he'd continued to pour all his energy into his work. The marriage had been over for a long while, if he was honest with himself, and when Chrissie had told him she wanted a divorce he'd felt only sadness at the wasted years. Em and Rob were grown up, his daughter with her own family and his son just returned from a gap year on a sheep station. Although they were sad about their parents' split, they were old enough to cope. All Mark had to worry about now was what meal to bung in the microwave and whether he watched the game or read a book.

The news of his father's fall had changed everything.

Mark didn't need to be a surgeon to know that a broken hip and pneumonia were bad news for a man in his eighties. Within twenty-four hours he'd been on the plane, then driving down to Cornwall and straight to the hospital. The sight of his father lying in the bed with the rails up, his hands curled like claws around the sheet and his mouth open as he slept under sedation, had shaken Mark to the core. John had always been larger than life and in Mark's mind he was still that man, the one who lifted feed sacks as though they were stuffed with feathers and who strode about the place with a brimming energy. How could this frail old man, his skin paler than the starched sheets, be the father he knew? It was impossible.

Mark sighed. When he looked in the mirror he didn't see the young guy he was expecting, either. Who was this middle-aged man with greying curls and lines starring from his eyes, and carrying a few more pounds than he probably should? His father's face stared out at him more and more these days, and his mother's worried green eyes were there too. An entire lifetime had passed by and if Mark wanted proof of this he only had to look at Rob. How was it possible that he had a twenty-year-old son? With his mop of black curls and tall rangy frame, Rob could have passed for the lad Mark had once been – although there any similarities ended. The suntan, chilled attitude and easy-going nature were pure Oz and the determination to make his own way in life was all Rob's. Unlike Mark (who, when he looked back with twenty-twenty hindsight, had been driven to his new life in Australia by hurt as much as by ambition and dreams), his son knew himself inside out and was sure of what he wanted.

Mark might not like it but his son was keen to drop out of going to uni. The gap year had stretched into two years and now Rob said he didn't want to study science at all but he did want to farm. There was an irony in this, of course. Farming was in his blood. Mark might have walked away and chosen an academic route but Rob, it seemed, was longing to pick up where his father had left off. Chrissie had said it was Rob's choice but Mark smarted with the sting of rejection.

Was this how it always was with children? You gave them everything you'd worked towards, offered them the better life that you'd made for them, only for them to turn their back on it? That was how it felt to Mark and, he was coming to realise, exactly how it must have felt to John. What Mark had seen as a huge adventure in a new and exciting land must have seemed like the ultimate betrayal to his father. At fifty-eight the world looked very different to how it had appeared at eighteen; it was only now that Mark understood how hurt John must have felt to see his only son reject the family farm. The Tucketts had worked their little slice of Cornwall for generations and Mark's future had been mapped out for him since birth.

Mark and Rob had talked on the long flight over and Mark was grateful for his son's company and support, as well as his willingness to shoulder the day-to-day running of the farm. With Rob to take care of farm business, Mark could concentrate on his father. At least the days of cows and pigs were long gone and all that remained were the sheep, which Rob said would be no problem for him.

"Where's the helicopter, Dad?" he'd asked when they'd arrived at the farm.

"Helicopter?" Mark had echoed, wondering whether jet lag had got to his son. "Why would Grandpa have a helicopter?"

"How else do you round up sheep?" Rob had deadpanned. Then he'd winked. "I'm messing with you, Dad! Unless Grandpa has twenty thousand acres you never mentioned?"

"Not that I'd noticed. Just two hundred acres, a dog and a Land Rover, from what I can remember," Mark had replied. "There's a guy who helps out too, I think. He lives in the village."

"Ripper," Rob had said, and that had been that. They'd literally just dumped their bags in the kitchen and then Mark had gone straight to Truro to see John, while Rob had taken care of the rest. His son had found the farmhand – nearly as old as John and even more deaf – and had soon located the sheep and a quad bike too. Once they'd both recovered from jet lag, Mark had taken his son walking up on the moors to show him the spots where their flock had always grazed. He'd been jolted by the harsh beauty of the place; in spite of everything, his heart lifted to see it again. It was true what they said: there really was no place like home, especially as you grew older. Australia had been a fun country to live in, particularly in his youth, but Mark was no longer a young man…

"Still here, boy?"

John's voice was cracked with exhaustion and pain but a familiar thread of iron strung the words together. Mark found himself leaning forwards with full attention.

"Still here," was all he said.

"What day is it?" John's weathered face was furrowed. "They don't tell me anything here. What about the farm? What about the sheep? I need to get home but they don't listen. Bloody nurses."

"It's Christmas Eve and the nurses do listen, Dad, but you've been pretty unwell," Mark reminded him gently. "The farm is fine. Rob and I are looking after it, remember?"

"I've broken my hip, not lost my marbles," his father snapped. His face taut with discomfort, he sank back onto his pillow before he sat up again, looking horrified. "Did you say Christmas Eve? I can't lie around here. I've got things to do! Grace will be arriving. She'll need her tree and her wood."

Mark's heart shivered. He'd known that Grace had inherited Hallows from her grandmother, and over the years he'd gleaned a few scraps of knowledge about her. His mother had always enjoyed a good chat; understandably, she'd assumed that Mark was long over his first love. Why wouldn't she think that? After all, he was thousands of miles away and had married someone else.

She'd been wrong. He'd never forgotten Grace. He'd loved her so much and thought of her for so long that she was a part of him. He would never be over her. Never.

"That's all taken care of," he said now, in answer to his father.

"How is it?" snapped John. "I'm here and you're here. She'll need her tree up and her Aga lit. She's a busy woman, you know."

Mark did know. He'd Googled Grace once in a moment of weakness. Her face had smiled out from the screen and across the years. Her eyes had been just as clear and blue as he remembered, and her hair was almost the same softly curling auburn – albeit silvered in places and pinned up, rather than tumbling to her waist in a shimmering waterfall. Even her on-screen smile had the power to make his breath catch in the way that it always had. He'd told himself it was just because he was alone again and feeling nostalgic for his lost youth, but deep down he knew that wasn't it. The simple fact was that he had never, ever loved anyone the way he'd loved her – not even Chrissie, so no wonder his marriage hadn't gone the distance. That Grace hadn't felt the same way was a tragedy Mark kept to himself. Grace's career was certainly every bit as impressive as he'd always known it would be and her formidable granny would have been so proud.

He was proud in a bittersweet and wistful way.

"Rob's doing the tree," he said.

"He's a good lad," John replied, closing his eyes again. "And you're not so bad either. A bit of a fool in some ways, but you're a good man. A good son to me."

This unusual praise brought a lump to Mark's throat and, as his father drifted back into sleep, he stared out of the window. He didn't see the heavy skies or the first flakes of snow begin to fall. Instead all he saw was a young man shouting at the girl he loved, then turning his back on her and striding away, closing his ears to her sobs and hardening his heart too. Then he saw his hands tearing up the tissue-thin airmail letters, the pieces fluttering in the hot Australian air like blue confetti as her words and thoughts and hopes were cast away to the winds as though meaningless. When the letters had finally stopped arriving he'd only had himself to blame.

His father was wrong. Mark wasn't a good man. He'd chosen to let pride keep him away from the girl he loved. He should have fought for her. He should have come home and told her how he felt. He shouldn't have wasted all those years with Chrissie either. It hadn't been fair on either of them. He loved the kids and he'd never regret them, but the years spent bickering and point-scoring hadn't been much fun.

He should have been the one to welcome Grace home this Christmas Eve, Mark realised, and every Christmas Eve that had gone before too – as well as every Christmas still to come. And as for a good son? Would a good son have let his father live alone like this, struggling to work a farm and returning afterwards to a cold and dusty house? Mark didn't think so.

It was Christmas Eve and he wished with all his heart that he could put things right, but it was too late now. Far, far too late.

Wasn't it?

CHAPTER 4
ISOLDE

Isolde's toes had lost all sensation and her eyes watered with cold. Every step she took across the moorland was a step closer to a cup of tea and a mince pie with Grace, she reminded herself, and each mile she covered burned a few more calories to offset her friend's delicious cooking. As she'd set out on her walk, letting the dogs off their leads so that they could bound ahead and sniff out all the smells in the heather, Isolde had told herself that there were still things to look forward to this Christmas. It was just hard to focus on them at times, that was all.

It was a beautiful crisp day and while she climbed the familiar track that snaked upwards to the summit of Hallow Tor, Isolde played the *counting her blessings* game. She'd come across the idea in one of her self-help books and, so far, it was proving to be the best way to counter the raw ache of losing Alan. Not that such a tearing, searing loss could ever be fully neutralised, but short of getting into bed and never getting out again (which Alan would have deplored anyway, since he'd been the kind of person who was always on the go) it was the best she could come up with.

My husband's dead, wept her heart. What a lovely sparkly frost, Isolde countered quickly. *I'll never see Alan again.* Oh look! A lovely buzzard! *I can't bear lying in bed without him.* Aren't you lucky to have a big warm bed when so many people are homeless? On and on this emotional tennis went until she was exhausted. It had been months now and Isolde knew that her friends and neighbours, although not exactly uninterested, had moved on and expected her to have done so too. Besides, they had their own problems. Look at poor John Tuckett, laid up in hospital with a broken hip and highly unlikely to be able to run his farm again.

Aren't you lucky to be fit and healthy!

And she was lucky, Isolde reminded herself as she lobbed a ball for the dogs to chase. She might be in her late sixties and ache a little, but she was lean from all her walking and fighting fit too. There was another blessing for the collection – and her drawing was yet another. Isolde's gloved hand slipped into the pocket of her red duffel coat, her fingertips brushing the sketchbook for reassurance. It had been too cold to take her gloves off and her wool-clad fingers had been clumsy but, even so, she'd managed to do several sketches she was pleased with. The buzzard soaring over Hallow Tor might be just the thing for a new painting.

Aren't you lucky that you have your art?

I'm getting good at this, Isolde decided. She could also throw in *Aren't you lucky to have a daughter who cares?* because Lizzie did care, even if she thought the few remaining marbles her mother had were rolling away.

"You need to move closer to us," was her daughter's constant refrain. "Come on, Mum. That place is too big and too isolated for you now Dad's gone."

Nobody could ever accuse her daughter of being subtle, Isolde reflected. Then again, you probably didn't become a successful saleswoman by holding back your opinions – and Lizzie was certainly successful. She met all her targets (*smashed them*, was her preferred expression), drove the kind of car teachers could only dream about and seemed to spend all her time shouting into a mobile. Lizzie phoned most days, probably to check that her mother was alive, Isolde thought wryly, and had all kinds of ideas about sheltered housing and granny flats.

Isolde sighed. Much as she loved her daughter, she sometimes secretly wondered whether Lizzie had been switched in the maternity ward.

"I'm fine," she would insist to Lizzie, rolling her eyes at the dogs and holding the phone away from her ringing ear. "I miss Dad, of course, but I'm absolutely fine. I've got my friends and neighbours."

"All miles away," Lizzie would shoot back. "Mum, I don't like to think of you there alone. What if something happens? Can't you come and live near us? They're building new warden flats now. You could pick one off-plan."

The thought filled Isolde with dread. Lizzie's smart new-build home on an exclusive executive gated estate was soulless and squashed next to streets of identical houses. There were no wide-open skies, soaring birds or endless moors to soothe the soul and Isolde knew that she'd shrivel away in such a place. She loved the engine house. It might be impractical and a little draughty, but she and Alan had poured their hearts (and savings) into it. Her husband was a part of the place too; although he might no longer be with her physically, Isolde still saw him in the painstakingly repointed stonework, the thick slabs of walnut worktop they'd chosen, the handwoven rugs and all the artwork. This was where she felt closest to Alan. There was no way she could leave. She knew she'd never survive away from here.

Isolde also knew that Lizzie wouldn't give up until she wore her mother down. Still, Lizzie was worried and Isolde hated being the cause of that. Lizzie had enough on her plate without having to fret about her mother too. Children shouldn't have to worry about their parents. That was back to front.

I'm lucky she wants to be involved, Isolde reminded herself and then laughed. Involved? *Fussing*, was what Alan would have called it with an indulgent smile. He was always softer on their daughter. Lizzie had been a real daddy's girl and Isolde's heart broke to think how much their daughter was hurting. Alan had been so good at reassuring Lizzie; he would have appreciated that it was just worry that made her sharp. Isolde understood this too, but at times it was hard to be on the end of that concern. It made her feel old and, what was even worse, like a burden.

Christmas had been yet another battle of wills, one which Isolde had won – albeit by the skin of her teeth. Lizzie and her husband, the serious and silent Daniel, were off spending it with his parents in Northampton and they'd wanted Isolde to come too. Just the thought of spending this first festive season without Alan away from their home and under the concerned gaze of her well-meaning in-laws had been unbearable. In response, Isolde had put her foot down so hard that her daughter had been surprised into agreeing that she was probably better off having a low-key Yuletide in Cornwall after all. As she gazed down at her beloved engine house, the bitter wind snatching her breath and stinging her cheeks, Isolde was filled with relief. Although she wasn't exactly looking forward to Christmas, it had been nice to spend a quiet morning pottering around and then venturing up here before walking over to Grace's for lunch. She could hardly wait to see her friend. It had been several months now and a good gossip was long overdue.

Talking of Grace, wasn't that her little yellow car pulled up outside Hallows? The plume of smoke rising from the chimney and the warm glow of lights suggested that her friend had arrived. Isolde's spirits rose like the smoke. There was nothing like the company of old friends. With Grace she wouldn't have to pretend that everything was going well or play the blessings game – and this thought came as a huge relief. It was exhausting having to paste a smile onto her lips and set her features in her best *I'm fine* expression every time she was in company. To sit quietly in the low-beamed sitting room at Hallows, curl her hands around a mug of mulled wine and watch the flames dance in the wood burner would be just wonderful. Grace wouldn't ask questions but instead would simply allow Isolde to be, which was what she wanted. She wasn't ready to vocalise her loss yet.

Should I have told her about John? Isolde wondered as she called the dogs to heel and began the downward path back to Hallows. She knew Grace was fond of him, but the fact that his son was here for Christmas complicated matters. Isolde only had the bare bones of the story; however, she knew her friend well enough to understand that Grace's broken heart had never truly mended. If she'd thought Mark Tuckett was staying next door, might Grace have stayed away?

"She needs to see him again," Isolde said to the dogs. "Don't you think? If she still loves him, then isn't there hope?"

Alan would have told her off and scolded her for meddling, Isolde reflected. Maybe he was right. Without him to steady her she found it hard not to let her ideas carry her away. Her paintings were bold abstracts, the big canvases slashed with vivid colours, whereas Alan's photographs had always been so measured and precise. Together they had worked, each complementing the other, and without him she feared that she would spin out of control, faster and faster just like the dogs' ball as it gathered speed down the hill.

"Too late now," she said to the tors and the surly sky. "Grace will just have to deal with it."

The path was uneven and, as she cautiously made her descent, Isolde envied the dogs' ability to bound and scramble ahead. It took all her concentration to cover the rough terrain. There was no way Isolde was going to risk taking a spill and landing up with a twisted ankle. Lizzie would have a meltdown.

Goodness but it was getting cold! Digging her fingers deep into the pockets of her duffel coat, Isolde squinted across the moors. Usually from this point the view across the heather and rocky outcrops was uninterrupted all the way to Liskeard, where a giant television mast stood sentinel over the moors, stern and grey by day and a pretty blur of red by night. As she looked across now, it had vanished.

Snow was sweeping across Cornwall.

The last place to be when snow fell was on the moors. Isolde knew the paths and had walked them in all kinds of inclement weather, but when the mast vanished she knew that she'd need to move fast. It would be so easy to get lost out here in the confusion of whirling snowflakes and shifting landmarks; the bleakness that was so filled with beauty could also prove deadly.

The windows of Hallows Farm were a beacon as the flakes began to fall. Soft at first, they melted on her face like cold kisses – but with every step she took the flurries grew thicker, and soon the shoulders of her coat were dusted white. The dogs were barking excitedly and circling round and around, their plumy tails wagging as they chased the snow. At least they were having fun. Isolde wished she could say the same. Every few steps she was having to stop and wipe her glasses, and that was costing her time.

She glanced over her shoulder at the path she'd followed. Already it was covered with a soft powder. No signs of her footprints remained and behind her Hallow Tor had been swallowed whole by whiteness. Isolde's heart clenched. She'd never seen such heavy snow in the five years that she'd lived here. There'd been the odd sprinkling, which had vanished like a dream as soon as the sun rose, but never anything like this. John Tuckett, who tended to look on the dark side of things, had always warned that this could happen, but until now Isolde hadn't had any idea just how disorientating the snow could be. She thought she was heading in the direction of Hallows but it was increasingly hard to tell; the warm lights of the house only appeared when the wind danced around to whip the flakes in a new direction.

Snow for Christmas.

Lord. This counting her blessings thing was starting to become a habit. Still, better to think this way than that she might become an ice lolly.

"Straight down," Isolde told herself firmly. "Then left."

Or was it right? For a moment she dithered, before plumping for the left. The path was steeper and there would be a ridge at the bottom to step over. But where was it? Had she gone the wrong way?

Confused, Isolde stepped forward – then cried out when, from nowhere, she tripped. Hands outstretched, she plunged forward, her knees smacking onto snow-veiled tarmac and her ankle turning over with such force that for a moment she thought she'd pass out with the pain. For a while she lay on the ground with her heart racing and her breath coming in short gasps.

You didn't hit your head! Aren't you lucky!

This was true but, as she tried to stand up, Isolde's ankle gave way and she crumpled back into the snow. Several more attempts were met with the same result. There was no way she could rise to her feet, let alone walk home or even as far as the Tucketts'.

There was nothing else for it: she was going to have to sit here and pray that someone drove by. She hoped they would come soon, before she froze. It looked as though she was going to be playing her own waiting game with the grim reaper.

"If you can hear me, Alan, send me some help," she called up to the swirling sky. "I'm not through yet, you old bugger! I'm not ready to give up!"

But there was no answer, only the soft whisper of the wind and the whirling of flakes from a sky the hue of clotted cream.

"Bloody typical," said Isolde, crossing her arms and arranging herself at the side of the lane in a hopefully eye-catching position. "You never were much use in a crisis, Alan."

She supposed all she could do now was wait. Wait and hope. It seemed to be the pattern of her life these days.

CHAPTER 5
POPPY

The snow took Poppy by surprise. She'd driven across this stretch of Bodmin Moor countless times but never before had it looked so bleak or so unwelcoming. As the flakes began to whirl, her Fiesta's wipers flew back and forth in a frantic attempt to keep the windscreen clear and her hands gripped the wheel tightly.

Maybe she ought to have checked the forecast before she left? That would have been the sensible thing to do, the adult thing to do, but she'd been so wound up after the argument with her father that all coherent thought had vanished. Ned Anders had that effect on lots of people though, to be fair.

Oh, it was so frustrating! Just when Poppy thought they'd turned a corner and that things might be all right after all, he'd had to go and say those things. It wasn't so much what Ned had said either, but how he'd said it. Her father was the master of making snide insinuations and then pleading innocence when her mother or Auntie Grace or even Poppy pulled him up on it. Usually he sulked in his study for a bit and then the matter wasn't mentioned again, but recently things had been different.

Very different.

Her father could say what he liked about *her*. Poppy was used to being the black sheep of the family. There was nothing Ned could say that he hadn't said before. The lacklustre GCSEs. The A levels that had just scraped her into university (and a red-brick one too, the shame), and then quitting halfway through because she was pregnant. When she'd dropped that particular bombshell, Poppy had actually thought she'd given her father a heart attack. His eyes had bulged, his face had turned scarlet and even though his mouth had been open no words had come out, just a ghastly popping sound. Once he'd recovered there'd been an unstoppable torrent of words; quite often they replayed themselves in Poppy's mind like some hideous echo chamber of paternal disappointment to taunt her during the small hours.

Throwing away your life, bringing shame on the family, letting us down, breaking your mother's heart.

That last accusation cut the deepest. Poppy adored her mother and would never do anything to deliberately upset her. Besides, what was her father on? Who deliberately got pregnant in their second year of university with the sole intention of upsetting their parents? That was bonkers. Failing your exams and running up a massive overdraft was surely sufficient. No way had Poppy intended to get pregnant, especially with a guy she knew wasn't in it for the long haul, but from the moment the second blue line had appeared in the test window, she'd known one hundred percent that she was keeping this baby. Her hand had fluttered in wonder to her concave belly and, although her heart had been racing with terror, Poppy had known in an instant that life wasn't just about her anymore. Everything was about the tiny person curled safe and warm and deep inside of her. So, her dad could say what he liked about Poppy, but if he dared say anything about Jack? Her hands increased their grip on the wheel as she fought to suppress her anger. That would be unforgiveable. Nobody said a word against Jack. Nobody.

Jack. A flood of love and protectiveness, together with that constant terror that had stalked her ever since the midwife had handed her the red-faced scrap of outraged humanity, swept over Poppy. She glanced over her shoulder to check all was well. Sure enough, her baby beamed back at her, a plump Michelin Man swaddled in a scarlet all-in-one, all smiles and golden ringlets. He was a happy little soul and when he smiled at her, a gappy two-toothed smile, Poppy's exhaustion and worries melted away. She was shattered and poor but she wouldn't have swapped this for the world. He was *everything*.

"Not long now, sweetie," Poppy said, and Jack gurgled and kicked his legs. "Soon be with Auntie Grace. She'll be pleased to see us. Not like mean old Grandpa."

Jack blew a raspberry in reply and Poppy giggled.

"I totally agree," she said, blowing a raspberry back. "We'll have a lovely Christmas here, you'll see. We don't need him."

Poppy really hoped Grace was at Hallows for the festive season because otherwise she was stuffed. The row with her father had been ugly and she'd swept out of the house in a rage, Jack under one arm with his legs peddling the air, and her bags under the other. She'd only come home for Christmas because her mother had promised faithfully that everything was going to be fine. Poppy would have happily stayed in Exeter. Her flat there was basic but it was enough, and she was able to work in a care home each morning while Jack went to a nursery for a couple of hours. The fees pretty much wiped out what Poppy was earning but it wasn't really about that: it was more about having a change of scene and meeting new people. Some might scoff at her spending her time with old folk, but Poppy loved their company. They had so much to say and there was so much to learn by listening to them.

"Are you really happy to spend the rest of your life wiping arses?" Ned had hissed – and it was this as much as anything that had finally made

Poppy lose her temper.

"I'd rather be wiping arses than spending Christmas with one!" she'd shot back.

How dare her dad say this? The people she cared for deserved her time and to have their dignity upheld. Just because she wasn't earning a squillion pounds didn't mean that what she did was worthless. Poppy loved her job. It wasn't one she'd ever imagined she'd do or enjoy so much but, like becoming a mum, life was taking her on some very unexpected journeys. Poppy had never considered a career in nursing before but now it was all she could think about. She'd already picked out the courses she liked the look of, explored the funding and childcare options, and started to think about the practicalities. Not right now of course, but Jack wouldn't be a baby forever.

She'd arrived at her parents' house in Plymouth filled with optimism and excitement for the future and eager to share her plans. She really should have known better. Of course, her father had poured icy water all over everything. He always did this. If she didn't follow him into the family business she was a failure. It didn't matter that the mere thought filled her with despair or that she knew in her heart that she didn't want to be an accountant; as far as Ned Anders was concerned the subject wasn't up for discussion.

Deep down, in the part of her that she didn't often acknowledge, Poppy wondered whether Jack had been a subconscious escape from all this pressure. Sometimes she was lonely, and she worried about finances constantly; she was also in a perpetual state of terror that she might not be good enough for her gorgeous baby. All the same, she'd never once regretted her decision to have Jack. It sounded such a cliché but he really was the best thing that had ever happened to her.

"You need to move back in with us," had been her father's opening gambit. "You can go back to college and pick up your accountancy studies, and your mother can help with Jack – can't you, Amy?"

Poppy's mother had nodded. Amy Anders adored her grandson and Poppy knew he couldn't be in better hands. For a few moments she'd been tempted. Moving back home would be safe. There'd be none of the financial pressures and it would be a return to a time when things had felt a lot less scary and complicated. Then her father had sketched out his plans for the next few decades of Poppy's life (at least up until Jack was sent to boarding school and groomed to take his place in the family firm) and she'd heard the prison doors clang shut. On paper, coming back home might be the best option but the reality was that she'd be back to dancing to the same old tune. Her struggles to find housing, sort benefits, get a job, make friends – in other words, her fight for independence – would all have been for nothing. The only plus point might be that she could start her nursing degree a few years earlier and be established by the time Jack started school. This was when she'd mentioned nursing and Ned had exploded.

Poppy blinked away angry tears. She wasn't going to make that mistake again. From now on she'd do things on her own and her way.

OK, so driving to her aunt's place wasn't exactly going it alone, but it was Christmas and Poppy wanted to be with family. Jack deserved family at Christmas. His father was long gone and his grandparents were brimming with disappointment, but his great aunt was always there with cuddles and wisdom. Poppy could hardly wait to see Grace. She wouldn't lecture or give advice; rather, she was a great listener and somehow whenever you spoke to her you ended up finding the answers anyway. Hallows would be filled with greenery, there'd be wonderful food and a big glittery tree to make Jack's eyes widen and, as always, an eclectic collection of interesting people would pass through. There'd be laughter and conversation and love. In short, Christmas at Hallows was everything Christmas should be. Her parents hadn't attended for a while, making excuses about the lengthy drive and other commitments, but Poppy recalled the times they'd spent the festive period at Hallows as her happiest ever, so turning the car in the direction of Cornwall had been instinctive.

She was starting to question this decision now, though.

In the couple of miles Poppy had driven since the first flurries had begun, the snow had grown heavier, its whiteness smothering the moors and obliterating all the familiar landmarks. The windscreen wipers were starting to lose the battle and the wheels felt uncertain on the road. It was treacherous and Poppy's heart skipped a beat. What had she been thinking, heading off like this with a baby in the car?

Poppy leaned forward and squinted into the whiteness. She'd spent so much of her childhood at the family farm and she would have said that she knew the place inside out. Summers spent with Grace, the coolest aunt anyone could wish for, exploring the twisty paths and the secret tufty places where the ponies slumbered and the buzzards soared, had shown her the friendly face of Bodmin Moor. However, it was looking very different now. She was pretty certain that if she carried straight along this lane, Hallows would be only a few miles to the left. Or was it the right? Poppy slowed the car; in the ballet of the blizzard she was no longer certain.

She would take the fork to the left, she decided. It was as she was putting her foot down on the brake that the car seemed to slip and slide away beneath her. With a cry of distress, Poppy tried to brake even harder and turn the wheel in the direction she wanted to head in – but the Fiesta had developed a life of its own and was spinning around at a dizzying speed. It was only a few split seconds but it was enough to make her feel as though her heart was about to burst with terror. When the car stopped at last, the white world was still turning.

"Oh my God! Jack!"

Poppy turned to her son, frantic to make sure he was all right. Luckily, the baby seemed to have enjoyed the ride and was laughing, his little white teeth flashing in his pink gums and his fat starfish hands waving merrily. He didn't seem any the worse for his ordeal.

The engine was still running and the wipers were swishing to and fro. Poppy took a ragged breath. She was shaken and, when she tried to press the clutch down, her leg was trembling so much that the car stalled. She realised then that she'd veered off the road and onto the grass. When she turned on the ignition and tried the pedals again, the wheels spun and spun. The Fiesta was going nowhere and panic tightened in her throat.

Oh God. She had to hold it together and drive them both to Hallows. They couldn't stay here. She hadn't packed any of the things they always said you were meant to have with you in a car in case of bad weather – torches, blankets, hot water, soup. What kind of mother was she? Ned was right: she was useless.

The sharp rap of knuckles on the window made Poppy jump. A stranger was standing outside in the snow, peering in at her with a concerned expression. The headlights from a black Jeep made a halo around him in which the snowflakes whirled. He was young and muscular and extremely tanned for Cornwall in midwinter. His hair, shoved under a beanie hat, was a mass of ebony curls. She saw that his eyes were an exact match for the sage green of his waxed jacket, and noticed too the pierced ear, the cinnamon sprinkling of freckles dusting his nose and the dark stubble that speckled his jaw. He didn't look like an axe murderer, she decided. In fact, in his Levi's and biker boots, the stranger looked more *Baywatch* than *Crimewatch*.

Taking a chance, Poppy wound the window down a fraction. At this, the stranger gave her a lopsided smile that crinkled his eyes and made his cheeks dimple. Suddenly things didn't seem quite so bad.

"G'day!"

An Aussie in the middle of Bodmin Moor and in a snowstorm? Had she hit her head?

"That was a nasty skid. We need to get you somewhere warm before the weather really closes in." He glanced over her shoulder and spotted Jack. "Hey, little guy! Shall we get you somewhere warm? You can't stay out here, can you, mate?"

Her son gurgled in delight at being addressed by the stranger but Poppy was wary. You heard all sorts of stories and Jack was no judge of character.

"Can't you give me a tow?"

The stranger shook his head. "This is a hired ute and it hasn't got a hitch. Worse than useless, eh? And my old man's taken the Defender, so I can't shift your car until later. Where are you going? I'll take you there."

"I'm going to my aunt's place. Hallows Farm?"

"Grace Anders is your aunt?" The smile grew even broader and although the air swirling through the lowered window was cold, Poppy suddenly felt much warmer. "I was there earlier sorting out her Christmas tree and eating my body weight in mince pies," he added.

Poppy laughed. "That sounds just like my aunt."

A gloved hand was extended through the window.

"I'm Rob Tuckett. My grandpa owns the farm next door."

John's grandson from Australia. Of course! Now the penny dropped.

"I'm Poppy Anders," she told him, shaking his hand.

"Hello, Poppy Anders," said Rob. "Now, before we freeze, how about we go to Grace's and get your Christmas started?"

Poppy nodded but, as she followed Rob, she couldn't help feeling that Christmas had already begun – with the arrival of her very own Aussie guardian angel, it seemed.

CHAPTER 6
GRACE

Once she'd got over the shock of thinking that Mark Tuckett had materialised in her sitting room, Grace had been able to laugh at herself for overreacting.

Of course it wasn't Mark! He'd be her age now – and as soon as she'd moved closer, it had become obvious that the man on the ladder was in his early twenties. He'd explained who he was in a friendly voice that had instantly made her think of teatime soaps and pop stars, and to cover her disconcertion she'd busied herself bringing in the Christmas food from the car. Then she'd filled Rob up with mince pies (albeit shop-bought ones for now), telling him she was extremely sorry to hear about his granddad and promising to pop into town and visit John. She'd done her best to chat normally, even though her heart was racing. It was only once Rob had driven away, in the same shiny Jeep she'd admired earlier, that she was able to collapse onto the sofa and take some deep, steadying breaths.

Mark was here. He was in Cornwall. He was next door again.

Grace's pulse fluttered. For the first time in almost forty years they were close to one another again, with only half a mile of muddy lane between them rather than thousands of miles of ocean. Of course, Mark had visited before, but his time with his parents had never overlapped with her stays at Hallows. Would she see him? Did she want to see him? And did he want to see her? What would they say? How would they feel? Would he think she'd aged terribly? If only she'd taken the time to have her roots done before she'd left London!

Oh! This felt like being a teenager again! So much for a quiet and peaceful Christmas in Cornwall.

"Stop being so ridiculous," she told herself sternly. "It's ancient history! He's got a grown-up son, for heaven's sake."

Shaking her head in amused despair, Grace decided to find something to do to distract herself. The mulled wine was heating on the Aga, the home-made mince pies and cheese straws were warming nicely and now the fun part was here: it was time to decorate the tree. Rob had chosen a lovely one too and it looked perfect with its twinkling white lights and deep green branches. This was always the part of Christmas that she looked forward to the most. Every bauble in her box of decorations had a memory and a meaning, from the glitter-shedding cardboard stars that Poppy had made at primary school to the Murano glass angel from an Italian friend she'd met on a demonstration. Isolde and Alan usually popped in about now to help her; Alan would be reaching up to decorate the higher branches and good-naturedly taking direction from the women. The trio would drink far too much mulled wine and usually Grace would have to take half the decorations off again the next day and space them out a little. As she hung a pretty golden heart, Grace reflected that it didn't feel quite right to do this alone. She'd wait for Isolde. Her friend would surely be here soon. It wouldn't be the same without Alan – nothing was, of course – but maybe they could make some new traditions?

Abandoning the tree-decorating, Grace was on her way to top up her mulled wine when the house phone shrilled and made her jump. It wasn't a sound she often heard at Hallows, since only a handful of people had the number.

"Why aren't you answering your mobile?" Ned snapped when she answered.

Grace suppressed a sigh. The passing years hadn't done a great deal to make her brother any easier to deal with. He'd been a demanding child and now he was a demanding adult. How Amy and Poppy put up with him was anyone's guess, although Poppy had done a sterling job lately of standing up for herself. Grace was proud of her niece because, knowing Ned as well as she did, she could imagine this wouldn't have been easy.

"There's not much signal in the house, remember?"

There was an irate tut, which suggested Ned did.

"Look, I think Poppy's on her way to you," he told her.

"Golly," said Grace, taken aback. She hadn't been expecting her niece. Not that this was an issue. Grace adored Poppy and she adored Jack too. It would be wonderful to have them with her at Hallows for Christmas. But shouldn't they be in Plymouth? Instinct told her something was up.

"Any reason why?"

"She's in one of her moods, of course. Took offence at something and went storming off. I sometimes wonder whether the girl's quite stable."

Grace was nipping this right in the bud. In her opinion Poppy was amazingly stable for somebody who'd spent years living with Ned. Most people would have throttled him by now.

"Nonsense," she said firmly. "I've met a lot of young people in my time and Poppy has to be one of the most level-headed ones I know. What did you say to upset her this time?"

"Nothing," Ned answered sulkily. "I just mentioned that she needed to think about her studies and a future career to support her and Jack. She came up with some nonsense about wanting to be a nurse and I said she'd be better off doing accountancy."

"Ned! For heaven's sake!" Grace was beyond exasperated with her brother and his blinkered obsession with trying to force Poppy into a career she had no interest in. "She doesn't want to be an accountant. I think she'll make a wonderful nurse. When will you accept that she's a grown woman and a mother? No wonder she's had enough of you."

"You sound like Amy," he muttered.

"Then listen to your wife for once, before you drive your only child away for good. Is that what you want? To lose her and Jack?"

There was a brief silence.

"No," Ned said finally. "Of course it isn't. But I wasn't calling for a lecture, Gracie. I'm calling because Poppy's taken Jack with her, which is utter madness."

Grace felt indignant on her niece's behalf. "Of course she's taken Jack. She's his mum."

"Not that! The weather. Haven't you seen the forecast? They're giving heavy snow for the south-west. It's already three inches deep here in Plymouth. Amy's in tears at the thought of them out in this."

Grace hadn't heard the weather forecast. Having been in a hurry to leave London, she hadn't taken any time out to listen to the radio before setting off – and as she'd driven west she'd indulged in an audiobook instead of Radio Four. Sure enough, as she glanced out of the window she saw the snow falling steadily. It was already settling on the stone wall hemming her front garden, and even the distant swell of Caradon Hill had been erased.

She felt a prickle of unease.

"Poppy's got an old Fiesta and I'm not sure how good the battery is," Ned was saying. Grace softened, understanding that it was only his fear that had made him sharp with her.

"It could cut out," Ned continued, "and then they'd have no heating. I think she really needs new tyres too, but you know what she's like. She won't let us pay for anything. She's too independent by half – it seems to be a bit of a pattern with the women in our family."

"That's not necessarily a bad thing," said Grace, and her brother laughed wryly.

"I suppose not. Look, could you let me know when they arrive and tell her that…" He paused and cleared his throat. "That I'm sorry? I love her and I'm sorry."

My goodness, it must be Christmas, Grace thought. Aloud, she promised to pass his message on. Once the call had ended, she wandered to the door and looked out in wonder at a world that was growing whiter and whiter by the minute. Grace couldn't remember seeing such a heavy snowfall. Thank heavens she had food and drink and logs. At this rate, the lane would soon be impassable – and without John Tuckett to clear it, they'd be snowed in.

She looked anxiously up the lane in the direction of the village, hoping to see a little green car approaching, but there was no sign of it. Neither was there any sign of Isolde walking through the snow. Her friend was certainly running late, and now that she'd noticed the weather, Grace felt worried. What if Isolde had slipped while out walking? Or fallen in the house? The older woman was as lively and as sharp as many people half her age, but even so…

This was *not* the way to be thinking! Of course Isolde was fine. She'd probably lost track of time without Alan to chivvy her, that was all. She'd have walked the dogs and then returned home and maybe started to read something interesting. There was no point calling her mobile because Isolde never bothered to charge it. The two women often joked that a couple of yoghurt pots tied together with string would be more useful.

"It's just a bit of snow," Grace said aloud. They had much worse snow than this in other countries – Canada, for instance – and everyone seemed to survive there, didn't they? This panic was a British thing, the only way people could experience the Dunkirk spirit in the twenty-first century. The road was still passable and the main roads would have been gritted. That young Rob seemed a capable sort and he had a four-wheel drive too. Besides, there were folk due at the holiday cottage who'd be passing by as well. It wasn't as though they were about to be cut off from civilisation! She ought to be more appreciative of this weather because it wasn't every year you had a white Christmas in Cornwall. Already the world outside resembled the scenes on the cards she planned to string up around the room. It looked absolutely beautiful.

In any case, Grace had a couple of extra guests due now, from what Ned had said, so she'd better make the house welcoming. This was Jack's first Christmas and she wanted to make it special.

And Mark Tuckett might pop by too. You never knew…

Smiling to herself, Grace selected some carols to play from her phone to the speaker. Next, she set about making sure the radiator was on in the spare room and that there was plenty of hot water for when Poppy arrived. Finally, she returned to the pleasant activity of arranging the decorations on her tree while the snow fell even more thickly. With the carols playing, the wood burner glowing and candles flickering on the mantelpiece, Hallows couldn't have felt more welcoming or festive.

Grace was humming along to *Good King Wenceslas* when, abruptly, the music stopped and all the lights flickered and died. She waited for a second for them to sparkle back into life, her hand poised over a branch in mid decoration, but the room remained plunged into eerie blue shadows as the snow fell outside and the clouds crowded in. The electricity was off and it didn't seem as though it was in a hurry to return.

It was time to fill the log basket, make sure the Aga's firebox was topped up and light a few more candles, Grace thought. Something told her that she'd be opening her door to quite a few visitors very soon.

CHAPTER 7
NICK

It was snowing. Really snowing, and at Christmas too! As the flakes fell, Nick felt like a kid again. London with all its pressures and problems seemed very far away. His heart grew lighter with every mile that took him closer to his holiday cottage and he knew that walking away had been the right thing to do. Thinking about Lisa hurt but, while he drove, Nick probed this pain and soon discovered relief was lurking there too. Relief and something that felt like excitement.

There was something about the long drive that freed his mind. The endless expanse of motorway had become almost meditative and Nick had found himself contemplating topics he hadn't dared explore until now. His career, his father's expectations, his passion for photography, his love of the countryside, the feeling of being trapped – all these spooled through his mind as the road unpeeled. By the time he was almost at Hallows Cottage, Nick York had made some important decisions.

Life was short and he wasn't going to waste another second living it for somebody else. It was time to have a big rethink.

The snow was growing thicker and Nick was pleased to see from his satnav that he was only two miles away from his destination. The car made light work of the conditions but, even so, negotiating the unfamiliar narrow lanes took concentration. He was looking forward to arriving at the cottage and having a well-earned cup of tea and some biscuits. He'd picked up some basic supplies from the last garage he'd passed but, knowing that the cottage came with a large Christmas hamper, he'd not bothered with anything else. There would be enough in that to feed him for a couple of days and Nick fully intended to check out the local pub for anything else. This week was going to consist of lots of walks over the moors armed with his camera, followed by a pint and some hearty pub grub in front of a log fire. Then, once his batteries were sufficiently restored, he'd start to deal with everything else.

Two miles had become one. Nick slowed because the snow was falling faster and he didn't want to miss a turn or shoot past his destination. The landscape was far more exposed up on this part of Bodmin Moor, and half-forgotten stories of the mysterious black cats with bright eyes and sharp claws stirred in his memory. It was so isolated out here that it wasn't hard to believe in the ancient folk tales. Several times Nick thought he glimpsed something crouched on a stone wall or racing across the field, but of course these were just tricks of the whirling snow and his overactive mind. Still, imagine if he actually managed to capture the legendary Bodmin Beast on film! That would be something else.

"You're losing it, mate!" Nick said to himself. Nevertheless, the thought made him smile and the rest of the journey passed in a very pleasant daydream about his work taking pride of place on the cover of *Time* magazine or in *National Geographic*.

The satnav was telling him to turn left onto what looked like little more than a farm track. Maybe Lisa's desire for a four-by-four hadn't been quite so daft after all. There was an irony! After all the arguing about why they didn't need one, the Chelsea tractor was coming into its own now and tackling the snowy surface with ease.

Slowing down and squinting into the flurries, Nick drove by an old farmhouse where the windows glowed with candlelight. Another house was a few hundred metres along but in contrast was in darkness. An old millstone propped against the wall bore the name *Tucketts' Farm*. Nick glanced at the paperwork strewn all over the passenger seat. Aha. That rang a bell. The holiday cottage belonged to the farm and although Nick had arranged the rental through an agent, the farmer was apparently going to let him in. He needed to call there and collect the keys, but he'd been told that a fire would already be lit in his cottage, the hot water would be on and the Christmas hamper would be waiting for him to tuck in.

Nick frowned. The place looked empty. He pulled into a yard filled with the usual farm paraphernalia and headed for the front door. Moments later he was back in his car and reversing out again, doing his best to avoid the chain harrows and old pallets as the visibility was growing worse by the minute. There was nobody in and there wasn't a key. Maybe he'd got this wrong and the key was at the cottage after all? Nick certainly hoped so, because judging from the pewter sky and the heavy clouds, the snow wasn't about to stop any time soon.

Hallows Cottage was only another half mile along the lane and it was every bit as picture-postcard pretty as it had looked online – but it too was empty. Although Nick searched every place where a key could be hidden, there was no sign of one. He was locked out, cold and lost for any idea what to do next. Get back in the car for a start, before he froze to death.

Back in the Range Rover with the engine running and the heated seat cranked right up, Nick began to thaw out. So he wasn't going to die of exposure, which was one problem solved. Now all he had to do was find out how to get into his cottage. It was only mid-afternoon on Christmas Eve. He tried calling the contact number he'd been given but the phone rang and rang and eventually he gave up. The farmer was probably out feeding the cows or something. Coming from London, Nick was a bit vague about what farmers did, but this sounded likely. Feeling more positive, he drove back up the road, fantasising about having a hot bath and opening the wine.

The return journey was slower because the snow was falling so thickly that it was hard to make out where the road ended and the moorland began. Flakes danced in the cones of yellow light thrown from the headlamps, descending faster and faster to merge with the plump duvet of snow already tucking up the world. Nick's eyes were screwed up against the whiteness. He had the oddest feeling that the world was being erased. Or maybe this was just his past and the snow was a metaphor?

Nick shook his head and was laughing at himself for these fanciful thoughts, when a burst of red amid the whiteness caught his eye. What was that? Not the Bodmin Beast, that was for sure – unless it had had a festive overhaul. Maybe Santa was early? Instinctively he slowed the car, drawing closer and closer until he realised that the scarlet splash was a duffel coat and the blur of red was a waving arm.

There was a person sitting in the snow, desperately trying to attract his attention!

"Oh, thank goodness!" said the red duffel coat when Nick drew up alongside it and leapt out of the car. "I was starting to think nobody would ever come by. John's in hospital and nobody else would need to come this way."

At least, that's what Nick thought he heard, but the speaker's teeth were chattering so loudly that it was hard to tell. Stepping closer, he saw that inside the coat was an elderly woman with long silvery-white hair and a face that had a dangerously blue tinge. Two springer spaniels were sitting next to her and looking up at him with curiosity. As he held out his hand to help her up they began to bark.

"Shhh, Pablo! Vincent!" she said. "Silly dogs! Do you want me to freeze?"

Her gloved hand took his and Nick helped her to her feet. She was as light as the snowflakes and as she pitched forward she gasped with pain.

"Oh! My blasted ankle!"

"Here, lean on me," said Nick, catching her elbow and stopping her from tumbling into the snow. Somehow he managed to help her into the car and load the dogs onto the back seat. Lisa would have a fit if she saw the paw prints on the cream leather, Nick thought, although she didn't have much right to object to whatever he did now.

"Oh! That's absolute bliss," sighed the stranger, sinking back into the heated seat while Nick made sure the full blast of the heating was aimed at her. "Thank you so much."

"No problem at all." Nick reached towards the back seat and pulled out the tartan car blanket. At last he'd found a use for the thing.

"I'm Nick, by the way," he said, draping it over her. "Nick York."

"Nice to meet you, Nick York. I'm Isolde Harper," said the duffel coat. "And you've already met Vincent and Pablo."

"Named after artists?"

"Two of my favourites. I was an art teacher and I still like to paint. I'm not in their league, of course, but I do love it."

Nick totally understood. "It must be great to be able to paint."

"I dabble really, my dear, but I enjoy it. It keeps me busy for hours. I was hoping to go sketching on the moors when the snow came in and I tripped. My husband would despair," she sighed.

Nick reached for his phone. "Can I call him for you, Mrs Harper?"

Her lips, slightly less blue now, curved upwards. "Isolde, please. 'Mrs Harper' makes me feel like I should be marking your homework. And no, love, but thank you for offering. My Alan's dead, although it might be fun if he answered! I'd love to know what he'd say. That I'm a silly old fool, probably!"

Nick wasn't sure how to respond to this. To laugh seemed inappropriate but Isolde Harper spoke with such humour that he couldn't help smiling.

"I'm so sorry about your husband," he said.

"So am I," said Isolde quietly. "Oh, so am I."

She closed her eyes for a moment and Nick watched her anxiously. She wasn't hypothermic, was she? He seemed to remember that you shouldn't let people go to sleep if they felt really cold, or was he just getting a bit muddled after watching *Titanic* far too many times? Lisa had loved that film.

"Do you need to get to the hospital?"

Her eyes flickered open. They were the faded blue of forget-me-nots, and filled with horror.

"I certainly don't! That's the last thing I need."

"But you've been out in the cold!"

"And now I'm in the warm," she countered. There was a steely tone to her voice that made Nick think of his old form tutor. The way Isolde was folding her arms and raising her chin suggested that she wouldn't be argued with. He could imagine the kids she'd taught hadn't been able to get away with anything.

Nick was worried. "You've hurt your ankle. What if it's broken?"

"Of course it's not broken! I've just twisted it. I tripped up. Honestly, it's fine. And besides, it's Christmas Eve and I'm sure you've got better things to do than drive me to hospital."

"Not really. I'm supposed to be staying in the cottage down the road for Christmas but I can't find anyone to let me in. There's no sign of the hamper I ordered either." He pulled a rueful face. "I've broken up with my girlfriend too, if you want the complete tale of woe. I'm starting to think this Christmas is doomed."

"I can't help with the girlfriend issue but I think I know what's happened with your holiday cottage," said Isolde. "The farmer who owns it is in hospital. His son's flown over from Australia to help out and I don't suppose he's got a clue about your booking."

"Great," sighed Nick. "I guess I'd better find a hotel then."

And then head home to London to sort out the mess of my personal life, he added silently.

"Absolutely not!" Isolde looked horrified. "Look, I'm warming up and I feel much better now, so let's forget hospitals for a minute and sort out some practicalities, shall we?"

"Yes, miss!" said Nick and she laughed.

"Yes, I'm a bossy old boot at times! Now, my ankle's twisted and since I live alone in a totally unsuitable house, at least according to my daughter, I'm going to have to ask a friend of mine for some help. She lives up the road and she always has an open house on Christmas Eve."

"OK," Nick nodded. This sounded like a plan. Hopefully Isolde's friend would know exactly what to do. He'd drop her off and then he could look for a room at the inn on Christmas Eve. It wouldn't be the first time in history such a scenario had occurred.

"Absolutely not," said Isolde again, when he mooted this idea. "Firstly, I owe you a big thank you and, secondly, if you had been able to get into your cottage you'd have found an invitation waiting for you anyway from my friend, Grace. She always invites everyone over on Christmas Eve, visitors and locals. She also lives next door to the farmer who owns your holiday cottage and I'm sure she'll be able to get in touch with him and sort out your key."

"I'm not sure," Nick said, feeling awkward. "I wouldn't want to intrude."

"Oh, you won't! Grace will be thrilled to see you. She's such a kind, interesting person and her Christmas gatherings are always wonderful. It's a mince pie, a glass of mulled wine and, with any luck, your keys. What's to lose?"

Nick thought about the empty locked cottage, a meal for one in a pub full of Christmassy people and the flat in London where his ex was probably celebrating with her new man. Isolde was right. There was nothing to lose. It might even be fun. It would certainly be different.

"Well?" Isolde asked.

Nick put the car into gear and smiled at her.

"Do you know what? It does sound like fun," he said.

CHAPTER 8
MARK

It wasn't easy to leave his father in the hospital on Christmas Eve, but the forecast of snow had proved to be extremely accurate and Mark didn't want to leave Rob alone to deal with the farm. His son seemed to have taken to it like a duck to water but, all the same, it didn't seem fair to let him shoulder everything. Mark recalled only too well just how much there was to do; even in its reduced state, there would still be a huge amount of work at Tucketts' Farm. He'd dithered for a while until the half-hearted flurries beyond the window had begun to fall in earnest, at which point he'd kissed his sleeping father goodbye.

The cold air outside had come as a shock after the heat of the ward, and the snowflakes had stung his cheeks. Although it was afternoon and the car park was still fairly full, it was noticeable that the locals were beginning to head home. Mark might have lived away for nearly forty years but he still remembered how quickly the Cornish weather could close in. As he drove away from the hospital, the spires of Truro Cathedral were already vanishing as the valley filled with snow.

Thank God his dad's Defender was up to the job of getting back home and through the lanes, Mark thought as he headed away from the town and into the whitening countryside. It was a shame it didn't seem to have a heater that worked though. His fingers were frozen on the wheel and his breath was puffing out in clouds. He'd found a hat and a jacket on the back seat, which should stop him freezing altogether, but it saddened Mark to think that his father had been driving like this – and probably for a long time, too.

Guilt clawed him. His father might say he was a good son but Mark knew the truth was very different. He'd hidden from his family because facing the past was far too painful. Look at him now, sending Rob to deal with Grace's tree and running away to Truro instead. He had no intention of seeking her out either. He'd lie low over the festive period and spend as much time at the hospital as possible. Then, once she'd returned to her estimable career, he'd think about what was going to happen to the farm.

They'd have to sell up, of course. That was obvious. John was frail and he wasn't coping. Maybe he'd be willing to move out to Australia and spend the twilight of his life in Cairns? Mark laughed out loud. The thought of his father kicking back on the deck with a tinny and wearing a sunhat was quite simply ridiculous. He'd be totally out of place. John Tuckett hadn't taken a day off in his life, and if anything would kill him it would be sitting around doing nothing and pining for Cornwall. Yet Mark knew there was no way his father could possibly manage the farm now. It could be months before he was home and, even then, there was a high chance he would fall again. And what if this time there was nobody to find him before it was too late? This thought gave Mark even more chills than the icy car. There were going to be some very tough decisions ahead and he didn't relish having to make any of them.

The car radio was working and, as he drove back to Tucketts' Farm, Mark tuned in to the local radio station. Already reports were coming in of traffic grinding to a standstill on the A30 and the forecast was of unusually heavy snow over the next twenty-four hours. It was something to do with an arctic blast from the north meeting mild wet air in the south, but the Met Office's words were interrupted far too often by his own worries to really take on any significance. Besides, they had enough oil and wood at the farm to last weeks – the old man must have been stockpiling it – and the sheep were pretty hardy. Rob had already taken some hay up to the feeder and there was enough long grass for them to eat. But if Mark, at fifty-eight, was cautious about venturing up onto the moors in poor weather, then how must his father feel?

Mark was humbled by this thought. In all their conversations John hadn't once complained or given his son any clues that life on the farm was becoming a struggle. He'd not wanted to be a burden and he knew how his son felt about the family farm. Mark sighed. What a Christmas this was turning out to be. As the snow grew thicker Mark yearned for the sunshine, the blue sea and his relatively uncomplicated life.

He was so wrapped up in these thoughts that when he turned left at the crossroads and found himself driving into Higher Hallows it came as something of a surprise. The journey had passed in a blur of snow and recrimination. Slowing to pass his old primary school and the Methodist church, long since converted into a holiday home, Mark was concerned to see flashing lights ahead. The emergency services? Out here in the middle of nowhere? Instantly he was in medic mode.

"Is everything all right?" he asked, winding down his window and flinching as the snow flurries blew into his face.

As soon as he spoke, Mark knew it was a daft question. Of course everything wasn't all right. The police wouldn't be here otherwise.

"It's all fine, sir," the policeman assured him. "It's just that there's a fallen branch causing an obstruction. It's taken the power line and the telephone line with it, so we're closing the road off as a precaution until everything's sorted out. I'm afraid that'll be a while though, seeing as it's Christmas Eve."

Mark peered past him. Sure enough, the power lines were dangling sadly from the post and the ancient tree where he'd once collected conkers was minus a big branch. The sudden weight of the snow must have been too much for it.

"I need to get through," he explained. "My farm is about two miles up the road. Can I pass by carefully or will I need to find another route?"

Mark didn't fancy this option one bit. The wind was getting stronger by the minute and the snow would soon begin to drift. The only other way to reach the farm was to take a lane that ran around Hallow Tor and came out near their Dutch barn. It was a rough route that was rarely used, except by the odd horse rider or trail-bike enthusiast. It would be a struggle to negotiate, even in a four-by-four.

"I can let residents through but there's no electricity beyond this point, sir, and there probably won't be for some time."

Great. Just great. Christmas without electricity. As if he wasn't missing Australia already! The policeman waved him through and the Defender pulled away carefully. The light was pearlescent and odd, the sky bulging with its unfallen burden. Mark shivered. Those people who dreamed of a white Christmas should be very careful what they wished for.

He made his way around the broken branch and progressed slowly towards the farm. Grace's windows were lit up by flickering candles; meanwhile, the engine house up on the hillside and the scattering of other houses over the moors were in darkness. Rob's hired Jeep was pulled up outside Grace's place, so presumably his son was still sorting out the tree and the logs there. She'd be fine with the wood burner going and the Aga. Unlike Tucketts' Farm, which was feeling distinctly unloved and un-festive, Grace's house was bound to be welcoming. He was sure that Grace would have been very busy getting ready for Christmas. His father had spoken about her Christmas Eve gatherings and, on his arrival, Mark had found an invitation on the kitchen table.

Open house at Hallows Farm! All very welcome!
Pop over on Christmas Eve afternoon for mince pies and mulled wine.
Season's greetings! x Grace x

Just a glimpse of that slanting writing had been enough to send Mark spinning back forty years. How many cards and letters had he been sent in that hand?

And how much did he wish he'd read them?

Mark had tucked the invite beneath a dog-eared copy of *Farming Today* and tried to forget its existence, which hadn't worked. Every time he'd walked into the kitchen he'd known it was there, daring him to lift the newspaper up and peek underneath for a bittersweet walk down memory lane. Well, that was one journey Mark wasn't undertaking. Absolutely not. He'd rather spend Christmas Eve alone in the farmhouse without electricity than do that.

He parked the car and let himself into the cold and empty house, determined that Grace Anders and his feelings for her were going to remain well and truly in the past where they belonged. It was too late for there to be any other option.

There was no way the Ghost of Christmas Past was paying Mark Tuckett a visit this year.

CHAPTER 9
GRACE

The first knock at Hallows' front door was followed by a shout.

"Grace! Where are you? Why are the lights off?"

"I'm in the kitchen!" Grace called, straightening up from lifting mince pies and cheese straws out of the Aga. "Come on in, it's unlocked! You know that! And I've no idea why but the electricity seems to have gone off. Not that it matters! We've got candles and the Aga and stacks of wood."

A figure appeared in the kitchen doorway. Isolde. In her favourite red duffel coat and flanked by her beloved spaniels. She was with a young man, who was dressed in a business suit and looking rather lost. For a moment Grace was thrown because she didn't recall her friend mentioning anything about a guest and she knew that Isolde only had a daughter. Recovering her manners swiftly, Grace placed the baking on the hotplate and wiped her hands on a red spotty tea towel.

"Happy Christmas! It's wonderful to see you!" Grace threw her arms around Isolde and hugged her. Goodness but her friend was icicle cold. "And happy Christmas to you too…"

"I'm Nick. Nick York." The young man held out his hand and Grace shook it. He had a firm grip and the eyes that looked into hers reminded her of sherry. He had floppy sandy hair and a shy smile, and she decided instantly that she liked him. Grace's instincts were never wrong.

Well, only once – and how was she to have known then that his *love* hadn't been love at all, but something far more conditional? She'd only been a girl.

"Nick's staying at John's holiday cottage but there's no key. I think his booking must have been forgotten, what with John being taken ill and everything," Isolde was explaining. She was leaning against the wall as she spoke and her face was taut with what looked like pain. Grace's heart clenched. What was wrong? Usually Isolde strode into the place, as bold and bracing as the cold wind that was now howling around the house.

"Please don't worry about that right now," Nick York told her firmly. To Grace, he added, "I found Isolde at the side of the road. She's twisted her ankle and she's very cold. Maybe we could get her a hot drink and sit her somewhere warm?"

"Stop fussing about me! I'm not an invalid!" grumbled Isolde, doing a very good impression of one as she limped into the sitting room with Nick and Grace propping her up. Before long she was seated by the wood burner with her foot up on a stool and her hands curled around a mug of mulled wine, while Nick tucked in to a bowl of soup with a sigh of pure contentment. The electricity was still off, but the candles and leaping flames from the wood burner filled the room with a cosy light and the pine needles from the tree added a festive scent.

Nonetheless, Grace was concerned. Isolde's ankle looked very swollen. "Do we need to get you to a doctor? What if it's broken?"

Isolde wiggled her toes. "It's not broken."

"And since when did you qualify as a doctor?" Grace asked.

"Stop fussing. It's just twisted and a bloody nuisance, nothing more serious. For goodness' sake, can you imagine what Lizzie will do if hospitals get involved? She'll have my house on the market and me in a home before you can say *Rightmove*!"

Grace didn't argue. In the past Lizzie had called her on several occasions, adamant her mother wasn't coping, and determined to persuade Grace to talk Isolde into selling up.

"I tripped, that's all," Isolde insisted. "I'm not senile and I'm not losing my mobility. It could have happened to anyone in that bloody blizzard. I just need a few days' rest at home, nothing more."

The engine house was beautiful but it was all steps and wrought-iron spiral staircases. The thought of her friend negotiating these hazards with an injured foot and no electricity was terrifying.

"You're staying here tonight," Grace said firmly. "I'll make up the sofa bed and you'll be toasty warm by the wood burner. The dogs can have some meat from the freezer and sleep in the kitchen. No arguments," she added as Isolde opened her mouth, "or I'll call Lizzie and she can deal with you!"

Isolde looked mutinous. "Fine, fine. You win. But what about Nick? He needs to get into his holiday cottage. Unless you're planning to kidnap him too?"

Grace smiled at Nick. "You're more than welcome to stay, and I've got plenty of room, but I'm sure you'd far rather be in your lovely holiday cottage. The farmer next door will have the key and as soon as his son's home you'll be able to collect it." Her voice trembled as she said this and Isolde shot her a worried look.

"Are you meeting friends?" Grace continued swiftly. Anything to steer the conversation and her own thoughts away from Mark.

"No, it's just me," said Nick. A shadow flickered across his open face, like sunshine over the moors when it played hide-and-seek with the clouds. "I've split up with my girlfriend. We were coming here together."

Instantly Grace's heart went out to him. Nick York's Christmas wasn't working out quite as expected. It seemed to be the season for it because

Isolde's certainly wasn't and her own peace of mind had totally evaporated ever since she'd learned that Mark Tuckett was home. It was taking every inch of her self-control not to fly to the window and see whether the lights were on at Tucketts' Farm, and her knees were all trembly at the thought of his proximity. *Get a grip!* she told herself despairingly. *You speak at conferences without any of this jitteriness! This doesn't make any sense.* But logic didn't seem inclined to care about her feelings. They may have been teenagers back then, but like everything she did, Grace hadn't approached their romance in half measures; she'd given it everything she had and she'd thought Mark had felt the same.

How wrong could you be?

"It's fine," Nick was saying, mopping up the last of his soup with a chunk of bread and butter. He sounded as though he meant this too, and he was looking quite cheerful for a man who'd just had his heart broken. "I mean, it isn't fine in some ways, but it's definitely the right thing. It's made me think about my whole life, actually, and what I really want."

"Sounds deep," said Grace, and Nick laughed.

"It sounds pretentious, more like! And this sounds even more pretentious but I'll say it anyway: I've decided I want to take some time out to do some photography. God knows how I'll do it but it's what I've always wanted to do, and why on earth not?"

"Good for you," said Isolde warmly. "Believe me, life's very short and we're really not here forever, so my advice is don't waste a minute." She held out her mug to Grace. "Talking of not wasting a minute, I've waited an entire year for your mulled wine and mince pies. Could I have a top-up, please?"

"I can see that you're going to have me running around after you now," teased Grace.

"That's the plan. You'll be sending me back home in no time," her friend retorted.

As Grace refilled the mug and shook some icing sugar onto the mince pies, the powder drifting down as softly as the snow outside, she listened to Nick telling Isolde how he felt trapped in his legal job and that his passion was landscape photography. This was followed by her friend's delighted reply that her husband had been a photography teacher.

"While you're here you must have a look at his studio," she said. "Alan loved to photograph the moors. A couple of his pictures won prizes and I seem to remember that one was published in *National Geographic*. He boasted about that for years!"

And, that easily, dear Alan joined the Christmas Eve gathering. His absence was still an ache but how wonderful for Isolde to be able to talk about him and pore over the precious memories. Her eyes filling with tears, Grace was just about to return to the sitting room when the back door flew open.

"Auntie Grace!"

In a rush of cold air and snowflakes, Poppy and Jack were in the kitchen. After Grace's exclamations over how much Jack had grown, followed by hugs and kisses and laughter, Rob Tuckett was also in the kitchen, standing awkwardly by the door. The similarity to his father was so striking that it was all Grace could do not to gawp. No wonder she'd been mistaken earlier on.

"Hello again," she said, recovering herself and smiling at him. "You seem to be in the habit of spending time with the Anders women today."

"Rob's been brilliant," Poppy said breathlessly. "My car skidded and he was right there, just like a knight in shining armour."

The sparkle in her niece's eyes said it all. Once again it seemed the Tuckett charm was working its magic on an Anders girl. Oh dear, thought Grace.

Rob was blushing at Poppy's words. "Aw. It was nothing. Anyone would have done the same."

Poppy spun around to face Grace, full of excitement at her adventure and her handsome rescuer.

"Honestly, Auntie Grace, I don't know what I'd have done if Rob hadn't found us. Jack and I were miles from anywhere and in the snow. It was like something from a film! Rob really did rescue us. He appeared from nowhere and brought us to you. I think he's our guardian angel! Can he stay for food?"

It sounded terribly romantic. No wonder her niece's eyes were shining. A snowy Christmas Eve dash from a grumpy father, then a skid in the car followed by a rescue thanks to a handsome stranger? Why, these were the very ingredients for a cheesy Hallmark movie and Grace laughed.

"Of course. I think the least your guardian angel deserves is some soup and bread. Or a home-made mince pie, if he'd prefer."

Rob looked doubtful. "I've got a bunch of things I should be doing on the farm and it's Christmas Eve. That's a family time and I don't want to intrude."

Catching sight of Poppy's stricken face, Grace said quickly, "It's certainly not an intrusion. You're very welcome to stay, Rob. I always have an open house on Christmas Eve and usually your grandfather comes over for an hour too. I'm so sorry he can't be here today but it would be wonderful if you could join us, even for a little while."

This seemed to set Rob at his ease and he nodded, accepting a steaming mug of mulled wine and a mince pie, which his strong white teeth bit into with enthusiasm. Before long, everyone was chatting away. In between fetching more food and drink, Grace listened to snippets of conversation and it seemed to her that some greater design was at work here; it was as though a plan was being woven through the words and laughter, a beautiful silver ribbon drawing them together, just as the heavy snow and the cut-off electricity had brought them to this very point in time.

There was Rob, with his passion for farming and so head over heels in love with the Cornish countryside and his family heritage – and, if she wasn't mistaking the glances that were passing between him and Poppy, there was something else here now to make him fall in love with England even more! Her niece, in turn, was talking to Isolde about how she wanted to be a nurse when Jack was older. Meanwhile Nick, who was quieter than the other two young people, was full of dreams about becoming a photographer and about to step into the unknown and a new single life. Then there was dearest Isolde, so bravely hiding her heartbreak and, judging by the wincing from time to time, also in no small amount of pain with her ankle. It seemed to Grace that their arrival at Hallows wasn't accidental at all, but part of something bigger than them.

Christmas magic, maybe?

"Is the electricity ever coming back on?" Isolde wondered. Outside, the twilit clouds were billowing in from the moors and the snow was tinged with blues and silvers.

"It's very unusual," Grace said. "There must be a problem with the line. Maybe a car's hit a pole or something?"

"I think it's beautiful," said Rob. "We don't have anything like this at home. England's awesome! I bet the doorknobs in this house are older than anything in Oz."

"But you have sunshine and beaches," Poppy said wistfully.

"We have beaches in Cornwall," Grace pointed out, but her niece pulled a face.

"Freezing cold ones, Auntie Grace! Brr!"

"No sharks though," said Rob, which ended the conversation fairly swiftly. Grace shivered. She loved swimming in the clear Cornish coves on hot summer days, but the thought of something predatory lurking beneath the water made her quail. It was another reminder of just what a different world Mark now inhabited.

Eventually, Rob said he had to go and feed the animals and he offered to let Nick into his holiday cottage. There was no hamper, he said apologetically, because neither he nor his father had known the cottage was booked. The beds might not even be made up. Nick protested that none of this was a problem and he was more than happy to kip on the cottage's sofa with a duvet, but Poppy insisted that she would get things ready for him while Jack slept. She helped her aunt pack a basket of food and even found some bed linen from the airing cupboard.

"My, you are being kind to Nick," Grace teased, at which Poppy's cheeks turned pink.

"I'm helping Rob, actually. He's got enough on with the farm and apparently his Dad's been acting all weird too. Rob says he's been really moody. He's not wanted to be near the place."

Oh dear. Grace hoped this wasn't her fault.

"He's probably worried about his father, love. Worry can make you act strangely sometimes."

Poppy rolled her eyes. "If that's a subtle way of telling me I should go easy on Dad, then it was pretty rubbish! Besides, since when has Dad ever gone easy on me?"

It was a fair point but, for her brother's sake, Grace tried again.

"I know he can be difficult, Pops, but he does love you and Jack. He was frantic about you being out in the snow."

Now it was her niece's turn to sigh. "I know, I know. But I've made up my mind about a few things and if he doesn't like it? Well, tough luck. I'm an adult now."

Grace nodded. "Of course you are. It's just hard for him to see that. It means he's getting older, and none of us likes that feeling much."

Poppy's answer was to give her aunt a hug. "You'll never be old, Auntie Grace!"

Grace wished that was true. Another reason why she was on tenterhooks about Mark being so close by was that she knew she was no longer the girl he'd left behind. She was a few pounds heavier now and she certainly never used to have silver in her hair or quite this many wrinkles. Generally Grace didn't worry too much about these things, but the thought of bumping into Mark made her reflect that the years maybe hadn't been as kind to her as she might have liked.

Oh! She was being ridiculous. She was heading for her sixties, so what did it matter? Cross with herself, Grace turned all her attention to making sure that Nick and Rob both knew they were welcome back at any time – including, if they wished, coming over for Christmas dinner too. When Rob said he'd love to, Poppy lit up like the Christmas candles, but when he then added that his dad would probably be up at the hospital, Grace was shocked to feel as though her own inner light had been extinguished.

Oh dear. She was used to being in control of situations and most definitely her own emotions, but this was something else…

Once Rob, Nick and Poppy had departed into the snowy twilight, Grace returned to the sitting room, where Isolde was watching Jack as he slept in his bouncy chair.

"He's a dear little chap, isn't he?"

Grace nodded. "He's adorable."

The light had faded and the room was now filled with pools of darkness and leaping shadows from the fire. After the chatter of the three young people, it seemed very quiet. The snow had stopped falling and all was still.

Across the world children would be waiting for Santa and, as she sipped her mulled wine and listened to the hiss and crackle of the fire, Grace felt the magical peace of Christmas wrap itself around her like a hug. Isolde must have felt it too because she was asleep, her head nodding and her eyes closed.

Isolde had had some day, Grace thought. Not only was her friend having to deal with the loss of her husband but she'd also had the fright of her fall.

Grace's own eyes were heavy and she must have dozed for a bit in the warmth, because when she opened them again Isolde was slumped forward on the sofa and groaning softly.

Grace was at her side in a heartbeat. "What's wrong?"

"It's my head. I feel so giddy, Grace. Everything is spinning."

"Did you hit it when you fell?"

"I don't know. I can't remember, but maybe," Isolde confessed. "Oh, Grace, I do feel strange."

Her face was a ghastly grey and Grace was instantly alarmed because Isolde never made a fuss. What if Isolde had concussion or had really hurt herself? A thousand horrible scenarios began to play through Grace's mind.

Grace wasn't a medic but she did know you didn't take risks with head injuries. But what could she do? They were miles from anywhere, the roads were thick with snow and the electricity and phones were still off. Her mobile didn't work in the house and who could she call in any case?

Isolde needed a doctor and, judging by the look of her, she needed one soon. As luck would have it there was a doctor nearby, wasn't there? A surgeon, to be accurate, and one who (as she knew from the few times she'd Googled him) was one of the best there was.

There was no time to be afraid or dwell on the past. None of that mattered.

Grace was going to go and ask Mark Tuckett for help.

CHAPTER 10
POPPY

"This is gorgeous!"

Poppy gazed around the small cottage. She wasn't sure what she'd been expecting to find but it certainly hadn't been gleaming oak floorboards, white sofas draped with cosy fuchsia throws and a stylish cream wood burner. She'd known John Tuckett for most of her life and she hadn't imagined that any holiday home he rented out would look like this. She supposed it just went to show you should never assume anything about anyone.

"I think the last tenant did all this in return for only paying peppercorn rent. It's a hell of a lot better than the farmhouse, that's for sure," Rob said. "Jeez, that's a bloody state. Grandpa's been camping in the kitchen and the rest of it's barely hanging together. We'll probably catch TB or cholera or something staying there."

"It's that bad?" Poppy asked, and Rob nodded his dark curly head. Goodness, but her fingers longed to touch those glossy curls. Alarmed, she took a step back. Not that Rob noticed; he was deep in thought about his grandfather.

"Yeah, it's bad. Grandpa isn't coping with any of it and I don't think he has been for quite a while, poor old guy. It's awesome he's managed as well as he has but he can't carry on."

"What will he do if he can't stay at the farm?"

"Who says he can't stay at the farm?" said Rob. "He's not managing to run it by himself but there's more than one way to sort that. I've farmed in Australia and this is a great little place. I like it a lot." He gave her a slow, green-eyed grin that did very strange things to Poppy's pulse. "And I'm liking it even more now. Why shouldn't *I* stay and give Grandpa a hand?"

"You'd give up Australia for here?"

He shrugged his broad shoulders. "There's no 'giving up' about it. This place has been in my family for generations and farming's in my blood. The old man might have wanted me to be a doctor like him but that was never on the cards. Farming is what I want to do, so why not farm my family's land? It makes perfect sense."

Fathers who wanted their children to follow in their footsteps were something Poppy knew all about.

"It's a great idea," she told him. "You should definitely go with your heart and do that."

"My old man won't be happy," Rob sighed.

"My dad isn't happy with me either," said Poppy. "He wanted me to follow him into accountancy but I always knew I'd be hopeless at that. I wanted to be a nurse."

"That's an amazing job. Good on you. So, are you a nurse?"

She sighed. "Not yet, but I'm going to do everything to make sure I will be one day. At the moment I'm a single mum, a care assistant and a total disappointment to him."

"Well, being a care assistant is pretty important too, if you ask me. I'm sorry to hear your old man thinks you're a disappointment, which I think is ridiculous by the way, but I'm very happy to hear you're a single mum," Rob said warmly. "Very happy, actually." He put his hands on her shoulders and Poppy's heartbeat began to race. She hadn't been this close to a man for as long as she could remember but there was something so open about Rob that she trusted him instinctively. Gentleness flowed from his soul through his fingertips and into her heart, and when he brushed his mouth against hers it felt like the most natural thing in the world.

Poppy closed her eyes and kissed Rob back, losing herself for a moment in the warmth of his lips and the delicious sensation of his arms pulling her close against him. She longed for more, to take his hand and lead him up the twisty turny staircase to the bedroom and see exactly where those kisses might lead, but then she remembered that Nick was unpacking his car and would return at any moment. Besides, there was Jack to think about too. She wasn't just Poppy Anders these days; she came as a package and it wasn't one that a man could take lightly. Jack was her world, and when and if she chose to let a guy close again, he'd have to understand that.

Slowly, she lay her palms against Rob's chest and pushed him away.

"Sorry," she said.

"I'm not. I've wanted to do that since the second I first saw you," Rob replied. His green eyes held hers and Poppy could hardly breathe as she stared into them. Did Rob mean that? He didn't seem the kind of man who would spin a girl a line. In many ways he reminded her of his grandfather: straight down the line, plain speaking and the sort of person you trusted instinctively to be there for you.

"Jeez, I can't believe I said that out loud." Rob raked a hand through his curls and his cheeks were stained red. "Do you know what it would do to my Aussie bloke reputation if anyone had overheard?"

"You'd better grab a tinny and throw a shrimp on the barbie fast then, cobber!" Poppy countered.

Rob laughed. "And then put my hat with corks on, right? And maybe wrestle a croc? I reckon you've watched *Neighbours* way too much."

"It's probably why you seem so familiar even though you're a total stranger," Poppy agreed.

Rob's eyes, serious now, still held hers. "But we're not strangers! I know this sounds crazy but we have met before, when we were kids. I've never forgotten you. We played in the garden all summer. Don't you remember? It was really hot and Grandma filled the paddling pool for us? We went to the seaside some of the time too."

Snapshot images flashed through Poppy's memory. Bursts of light, noses red from the sun, lurid Fab ice lollies, a floppy sun hat, the smell of Uvistat sun cream, splashing in the water with a friend…

"I do remember! But we must have been about three!"

"Five actually," said Rob. "I'd come over with my sister for a month. My parents did London and Dad was lecturing somewhere, so they dropped us off with my grandparents. You were next door with your mum and dad, having a family holiday."

Poppy nodded. This had to be one of the last times they'd spent an entire holiday at Hallows. Her father hated the countryside and was usually itching to leave within ten minutes of arriving. Her childhood holidays had been mostly city breaks filled with museums and cultural visits. She fully intended that Jack would grow up on the beach and fill his summers with rock-pooling, crabbing and dripping ninety-nine ice creams – in other words, doing all the things she had enjoyed doing with her granny and with Grace. Of course, Rob had been there too that summer, a nut-brown playmate who knew how to catch shannies and climb rocks. If she dug out the right photo album he'd be there, forever five in faded Polaroid.

"So you do know me. I'm probably your oldest friend, if you want to get technical about it! So, how about a game of doctors and nurses? Just for old times' sake?"

Poppy swatted him on the arm. "I tell you my dearest dream and you take the piss?"

Rob placed his hand on his heart. "Never. I was being serious. Ouch!" he cried as she swatted him again. "About your career, not the other thing, although actually that too! But seriously, I'm not messing with you, Poppy. As soon as I saw you again I knew how I felt – and I'm sorry if this sounds mad, but I'm not good at playing games. I guess I'm just a simple Aussie bloke who says it like it is. This feels right, Poppy."

Poppy was touched and also relieved. The attraction she'd felt for Rob had been instantaneous. Was she recalling on some unconscious level their childhood friendship? Or was there really such a thing as love at first sight?

"Rob, I feel the same way but it's complicated," she began, but he stopped her words with a butterfly-soft kiss.

"There's Jack," he whispered against her lips. "I know how important he is and that he'll always come first – and that's fine. That's how it should be, OK? He will always, always be your priority. No matter what happens or doesn't happen. It's your call. If this feels too much or too soon then tell me and I'll step away."

The night had wrapped itself around the moors and the snow had stopped. The world was muffled and quiet. In the half-light, all Poppy could hear was her ragged breathing and the racing of her heart. Was it too much too soon? In some ways yes, in others no because it felt as though she had known Rob forever. Being in his arms felt like coming home.

She looked up at him. "It feels just right to me too."

"Oh sorry!" Nick had walked into the kitchen, rucksack over his shoulder, and stopped dead in his tracks. "I didn't mean to interrupt."

"You haven't at all, mate," said Rob. He smiled at Poppy. "We've got all the time in the world. Seeing as I've not been a very good host so far, the least I should be doing is helping you in with your luggage."

"This is my luggage. I left in a bit of a hurry," Nick replied, setting his bag down. "I'm not even sure if I'm going back, to be honest. I was thinking of quitting everything in London and starting afresh."

"It seems to be a bit of a common theme," said Rob. "I've decided that I'm going to stay here and help my grandfather run the farm. Fancy a job?"

Nick stared at him. "You're joking, right?"

"Nope," said Rob. "I'm going to need all the help I can get. Grandpa won't be on his feet for months and the farmhand's ancient, so I daren't ask him to do too much. You don't want to go back to the city, you like the country and you're single now, so why not?"

"But you don't know me."

"Did you holiday here when you were five, by any chance?" asked Poppy, raising an eyebrow at Rob, who laughed.

"She's playing with me," Rob said to Nick, who was understandably looking confused. "I guess I'm an impulsive kind of person, but I know when I like someone and you seem like a decent guy. You certainly helped Mrs Harper out today."

"Anyone would," Nick answered.

"No they wouldn't," said Rob. "Sure, they'd have picked her up and dropped her off somewhere, but they wouldn't have stuck around to make sure she was OK or talked to her about art and photography. And most folk who couldn't get into their holiday home would have been going crazy by now."

Nick shrugged. "It's hardly the end of the world."

"Exactly. Don't sweat the small stuff," Rob agreed. "Look, I don't know much about you, mate, only what you said about not liking your job and wanting to be a photographer. Seems to me like Fate is giving you a second chance at that. Come and lend us a hand on the farm and you can stay here and I'll do my best to pay you. It won't be very glamorous, mostly shovelling crap and lifting stuff, but you'll be able to be here, on the moors, and take all the pictures you want."

Nick was nodding slowly. "I need teaching though. I don't just want to snap away."

"Isolde used to be an art teacher and her husband was a photographer," Poppy recalled. "I bet she could help you and it would be brilliant if she had somebody to keep an eye on her every day. Maybe you could sort something out? You could do some DIY or chop her logs in return for art lessons?"

"You two seem to have it all figured out!" Nick laughed.

Rob took Poppy's hand, twining his fingers with hers and tracing tender circles on her palm that made her insides shiver.

"It feels like everything's coming together tonight. Maybe it's Christmas magic?" he said.

"You could be right," Nick agreed. "I think I may well take you up on that offer. After all, who am I to question the Christmas magic?"

The room was dark now and outside the snow had started falling again, soft flakes kissing the drifts that had settled like pluffed-up pillows on the windowsills and hedges. Poppy wasn't a child anymore but, as she held Rob's hand and watched the snow, she felt sure there really was something magical in the air this Christmas Eve.

CHAPTER 11
MARK

The snow was still falling when Mark arrived back at Tucketts' Farm. He parked the Land Rover in the yard and let himself into the kitchen, wincing because it wasn't much warmer in here than it was in the car. If anything, it felt even colder. Not for the first time since he'd arrived back in the UK, Mark felt a pang for his adopted homeland. What he wouldn't give now to be sitting out on the deck in the sunshine.

There was no chance of any warmth in the farmhouse this afternoon, unless he got to grips with lighting the range. It was a big cast-iron beast, which Mark remembered well from his childhood. Back then it had been the heart of the Tuckett family home, where Elsie Tuckett's nourishing stews had bubbled away, loaves of bread had baked to a golden crust and sometimes poorly lambs could be found snuggled up in the gentle heat of the oven. There had always been tea towels drying on the rail, along with socks and jeans airing on the wooden rack above. Usually somebody would be leaning against the range, thawing out after a long day working the farm or a chilly walk over the hill to visit friends.

The kitchen of Mark's childhood bore no resemblance at all to the unwelcoming room he was standing in now. Christmas Eve had always been an especially busy time with all the preparations for the big day taking place. As he crammed logs into the firebox, Mark recalled how his mum had spent hours scoring crosses into the bottoms of sprouts (for reasons that still escaped him), her hands red and raw from the icy water; she'd spent even longer peeling potatoes and making stuffing. Elsie Tuckett would never have dreamed of turning to Aunt Bessie for help or nipping to the shops for some ready-made extras. The thought would have horrified her. In Elsie's kitchen, everything was always made from scratch and using produce from the farm. The only thing that hadn't been made by his mother, Mark remembered, was the mincemeat for the mince pies: this had always been a gift from Mary Davies next door to them at Hallows Farm.

Mark struck the match and sat back on his heels to watch the fire take hold. Once the Rayburn was lit, he'd keep it fed with the logs he and Rob had chopped and the house would soon be warm. As the flames licked over the dry wood, his memories began to catch too, spreading through his mind's eye with all the speed and intensity of a forest fire. How was it that a man could be away from a place for almost all his life, and do his very best to put the past behind him, and yet find that within just days of returning the memories were as vivid as though the events had happened only yesterday? It was an emotive time of year, he told himself firmly, and seeing his father so frail and so poorly in the hospital was bound to have an effect. Life on the farm hadn't been all bad and there were lots of good recollections of it too – many of which were associated with Christmas.

One year they'd reared turkeys, huge and ferocious birds with sharp beaks and crimson necks, which had terrified Mark when he'd been sent to feed them. They'd grown so big that it had taken the combined strength of both his parents to cram their chosen bird into the oven, and Elsie had joked that they'd all be eating turkey until Easter. Not that there'd ever been any likelihood of that, given the number of mouths to feed. Every seat at their big kitchen table was always taken for Christmas dinner. There were the farm workers and their families, plus neighbours like Mary from Hallows. Sometimes the Methodist minister joined them too – and then there were Mark's grandparents, who had lived with them. There had been laughter and noise and fun, and he felt a twist of sadness that those days were gone forever. It would be a quiet Christmas this year with just him and Rob, and rather than the feast of bygone years they would be dining on microwave curries. If he listened carefully enough, Mark would probably hear the rumbling of his mother turning in her grave.

Elsie Tuckett would also be furious if she could see the state of the house, Mark reflected. The cold and damp place he'd returned to was nothing like the happy home he remembered. His mother had been a proud housekeeper – but without her to keep on top of the chores, dust and grime had slowly reclaimed the place, inch by inch. This creeping but determined advance of dirt inside the house was mirrored by the weed-choked vegetable patch and flower beds outside it, which could have given the Lost Gardens of Heligan a run for their money.

Deep in thought, Mark filled the kettle and placed it on the hotplate. That shouldn't take too long to warm up and at least he could have a cup of tea. The microwave meal was out for the moment though; he would have to wait for the electricity to come on for that. The radiators would take a bit longer to heat up, so until then he supposed he would have to huddle in his coat and eat his own body weight in custard creams, since these were all John appeared to have in the larder (unless he really wanted to risk opening some corned beef that pre-dated the Falklands War). As for lighting? At least the ancient hurricane lamps his parents had kept in case of power cuts were still stored behind the moth-eaten deckchairs in the porch. There was a can of paraffin too, so he'd be able to light the kitchen as he made tea and ate biscuits, while still wearing his coat and hat.

It wasn't quite the Christmas Eve he'd had in mind.

Outside, the daylight had finally surrendered to dusk's advance. The snow had stopped falling and stillness had settled across the violet countryside, as though the world was holding its breath before the coming of the Christ Child. Recalling how his mother had always told him that at midnight all the animals would kneel down in reverence, Mark's throat tightened. Elsie might have been gone for over a decade but these little memories always clawed his heart with unexpected grief. Maybe this melancholy was part of getting old? The years had slipped away from him so smoothly that he'd barely even noticed, until it had occurred to him that the dear faces he'd taken for granted were no longer there. This year there would be far too many empty seats at the Christmas table; instead of conversation filling the place, Tucketts' Farm would echo with *what ifs* and *if onlys*.

Lord! It was the solitude and the season that were getting to him, that was all. But even as he thought this, Mark knew it wasn't the case. If the sun had been blazing down from a brutally blue sky and he'd been flipping steaks on the grill, he wouldn't be feeling like this, even if he'd been alone and on the other side of the world. It was being back in his childhood home, cast adrift on an ocean of memories, and being forced to face the fact that something had to be done to help his father. It was these things that were making him nostalgic and a little blue, that was all.

Well, this and the knowledge that the girl he'd once loved was nearer now than she'd been for almost forty years. Mark sighed. The temptation to pull on his wellies and walk over to Hallows was becoming stronger by the moment. He hoped Rob would return soon and distract him. Maybe they would walk back to the village and have a few beers and some food in the pub? The thought of tucking into steak and kidney pie, chips and a pint was a welcome one. It would feel festive too because, unlike the bleak farmhouse, The Hallows Inn was big on fairy lights all year round, from what Mark remembered of it. At least the electricity was on in the village. He wasn't quite sure how you cooked a microwave meal in a Rayburn.

Eventually the kettle boiled and he made himself a cup of tea and drank it at the kitchen table, thinking about the hard decisions that would have to be made in the coming weeks and dreading being the one to make them. The table was littered with letters from the local GP, all of which his father must have ignored. As Mark read them now through his medic's eyes, he felt his spirits sink further. There was information about high blood pressure, together with repeat prescriptions for medication that John wasn't bothering to take, judging by all the unopened packets stuffed under the sink. There was also one very worrying letter asking why John hadn't attended an MRI scan. Then there were the red bills and the council tax reminders, also bundled away out of sight, and the demands from the feed merchants for payment. The bank statements Mark had located showed a shockingly healthy balance, which concerned him even more. His father, a stranger to the new-fangled worlds of telephone and internet banking, wasn't leaving the bills unpaid because of a lack of money but probably because he couldn't face driving to town.

If John Tuckett was unable to drive then there was no way he could live in isolation out here on the moors. He certainly wouldn't be able to drive for months now, and he was going to need care. Mark was going to have to tell his father that the family farm needed to be sold.

There was a lump in his throat. This was going to be the hardest thing he'd ever had to do. Leaving home, getting divorced, even losing Grace, were nothing in comparison to telling John that he couldn't stay at the farm. Mark knew that leaving this place would break his father's heart. He was going to be the one responsible for causing that heartbreak: it was his failure to follow in his father's footsteps that had brought them to this moment, and Mark didn't think he could bear it.

"I wish you were here, Mum," he said out loud. Almost sixty and he still needed his mum – but then, didn't everyone in the end? Everyone longed to be accepted, to be wanted and loved no matter what they did, to be thought perfect in somebody's eyes. Without his parents, who would ever feel that way about him again? Lovers had come and gone, including his wife, and Mark knew that his children had their own lives to lead now. It was exactly what he wanted for them, of course, but the loneliness sometimes felt overwhelming. What was the right thing to do for John? How would he ever know for certain? The room blurred and swam for a minute because there was nothing he wanted so much right now as a hug from his mum. He craved her unconditional love and its promise that, no matter what he did, no matter what choices he made, she would always be there.

Without really knowing why, he picked up one of the hurricane lamps and climbed the stairs, coming to a halt beside his father's bedroom door. Mark stepped into his parents' bedroom and it was immediately apparent that John Tuckett hadn't slept up here for a very long time. The same candlewick bedspread he remembered from his childhood was covering the bed, tucked in neatly at the headboard. A chenille throw was draped over the foot of the bed and two matching cushions sat jauntily on the pillows. He cast his eye over the dusty dressing table and noticed the bottle of long-evaporated perfume, beside which slumbered a dried-up lipstick and a hairbrush with a few silver strands still coiled in its bristles.

Mark raised his arm and the lamp threw leaping shadows across the room, illuminating the pictures arranged on the bedside table and revealing their tarnished frames. There, frozen forever in time, were the memories Elsie had treasured and looked at every day for a lifetime: the wedding photo of her and John, impossibly young and hopeful with linked arms and nervous smiles, captured in black and white glory; Mark as a plump baby with dimpled wrists and one tooth; images of Mark on his bike, at a football match, at a dance with Grace, opposite the opera house with Chrissie; his own children playing in the farm's sunny garden with another small girl; pictures of their first days at school; Rob's graduation; Em's christening…

Again, there was a lump in Mark's throat. Sending these photos had been such a simple thing for him to do, almost a throwaway gesture, but it had meant the world to Elsie. It didn't seem like nearly enough and as he looked at them now, in a room his father couldn't bear to sleep in and most probably couldn't even climb the stairs to reach, Mark felt dreadful. He walked to the window and leaned against the sill with his forehead resting on the cold glass. The sky was clear and sprinkled with stars, and the small slice of moon made the snowy hills sparkle like a thousand sequins.

"I wish I knew what to do, Mum," Mark said quietly. "I wish I could make things right this Christmas. I wish you could help me."

But there was no answer, just the misting of the cold glass as his breath warmed the chilly pane. He gazed at the distant, twinkling stars – as out of reach as his long-lost hopes and dreams. They must have shone this brightly two thousand years ago, he thought, and this idea cheered him. It was comforting to imagine that, for as long as there had been people in the world, they'd looked up at the sky and made wishes. Maybe some of them had even come true? You never knew.

A violent knocking on the front door put an end to these thoughts.

Why's Rob trying to come in this way when he knows we use the back door? Mark wondered as he headed downstairs again. How typical of his son to insist upon doing things his way. Then again, this was probably just what John had said about him. Maybe he had more in common with his father than it seemed.

"Can't you use the back door?" he grumbled, yanking the front one open. "You know we don't use the—"

Mark's words froze in the cold night air when he saw who was on the doorstep.

It wasn't possible, surely?

"Thank God, you're here, Mark!" gasped Grace Anders, her blue eyes wide and shimmering with worry. "You've got to come to Hallows now! My friend's been taken ill and I don't know what to do! I really need your help."

CHAPTER 12
GRACE

How was it possible to travel back in time faster than you could take a breath? As she'd walked down the lane to Tucketts' Farm, with Jack fatly swaddled in his all-in-one suit and riding happily on her hip while she shone her torch into the dusk, Grace had given herself a stern talking to. There was no need for her heart to flutter or for her knees to feel wobbly. Anyway, these things were simply caused by the speed at which she was striding along the lane and had absolutely nothing to do with knowing she was only minutes away from seeing Mark Tuckett again.

"Your great auntie's being very daft," Grace had said to Jack. "Silly old fool! He probably won't even remember me anyway!"

He certainly wouldn't recognise her, she thought sadly. The last time Mark had seen Grace she'd been in her teens and looked a lot like Poppy. Whenever she saw her niece, Grace was reminded of the girl she'd once been and still was in her heart – it always came as a surprise to look in the mirror and see the lines in her face and all the grey hairs. She still had an impressive mane of hair, but these days it was pinned up in a bun rather than tumbling to her waist in a riot of auburn ripples. She wasn't eight stone anymore either, and she'd stopped wearing flares too. Times had changed and she wasn't eighteen now.

Grace's mental lecture, delivered as she crunched and slithered her way along the snowy lane, went something along the lines of reminding herself that whatever it was she had shared with Mark was just teenaged nonsense and no big deal. Weren't emotions always more intense and heightened when you were that age and the world was all new and brimful with possibilities? Look at Romeo and Juliet! Three days of drama and then dead for love. On the face of things this all seemed very romantic, but she couldn't help thinking that if the star-crossed lovers had been together much longer Juliet would have been driven mad by Romeo's flowery words and lack of action, and his wandering eye would soon have lighted upon another. If they'd also had to contend with bills, housework and fishing dirty socks out from behind the sofa, they'd have lasted a year, tops!

So. It stood to reason that it would have been the same for her and Mark. Those emotions were strong at the time but would they have lasted? Statistically, probably not. It was just a first romance and, because she'd never found anyone who'd matched up to Mark since, her memory had built it up into something that was far more significant than the reality. It was quite likely he barely remembered her at all.

"It was just a childhood thing. It wasn't real," Grace told Jack.

The trouble was, she could tell herself this as much as she liked but it hadn't felt meaningless at the time. She'd grown up spending her summers in Cornwall with her granny – and Mark had always been there, as much a part of the place as the rough stone walls and prickly moorland grass. When they were younger he'd shown her the places where the sparrowhawks soared and he'd taught her how to skip stones across the village pond. He'd been her scraped-kneed, freckle-nosed partner in crime and together they'd scrumped apples from the vicar's garden, wandered for hours on the moors and squabbled over licking the mixing bowl in Elsie Tuckett's kitchen. Grace hadn't really thought that much more about Mark from one visit to the next. He was just the boy next door.

But this had all changed in the summer of her eighteenth birthday, during the holiday she'd spent at Hallows before going to Oxford. Exhausted from studying so hard, Grace had planned on spending her summer reading for pleasure, sunbathing in the garden and helping her grandmother. She might even catch the bus to Looe and enjoy the beach. The days had been hot and sunny, she'd worn shorts, sandals and a gingham shirt tied up under her bust, and her body had turned a delicious golden brown. Mark, the same age as her and dreaming of being a doctor, had been kept busy working on the farm. Now that they were older, their paths rarely crossed. Sometimes Grace had spotted him in the field or driving the tractor along the lane, but apart from that she'd barely seen him – and when she had, she'd found it hard to equate this muscular young man with her gangly playmate of yesteryear. Whenever she'd felt his green-eyed gaze settle on her, Grace had blushed and studied her red painted toenails until the moment passed. She wasn't sure why, but she was always sorry when it did.

The harvest home was always the local folks' highlight of the summer. The days were still long and light but the fields had been shorn and the hay baled. By then, the promise of autumn was in the cooler mornings. Each year, the Tucketts held a celebration in their barn and the whole village attended. There was dancing and food and cider for the adults (although on one occasion Grace and Mark had tried a glass and spent most of the harvest home fast asleep) and the party went on into the small hours.

That August, the hot summer of her eighteenth year, Grace had found that she was spending longer than usual getting ready for the party. In the past, she'd worn her jeans or a simple skirt, but this time she'd been to Truro and found a green dress with a pretty pattern of white daisies embroidered all over it and skirts that swirled when she moved. She'd left her hair loose; she was secretly very proud of her long red curls and felt that maybe they went some way to making up for her lack of height. However, she'd spent ages in the bathroom trying to paint her face. She'd been copying the make-up from a magazine, but what looked good on the model just made her look like a clown. In the end she'd scrubbed it all off in frustration and settled for a quick sweep of mascara and some lip gloss.

The party had been in full swing when Grace and her grandmother had arrived. She'd spotted Mark straight away at the far side of the barn, where he was talking to some other young men. He'd stood out a mile with his shoulder-length dark curls, white shirt and blue jeans, and when he'd looked over and met her gaze the world had stood still.

"Oh, he doth teach the torches to burn bright," she'd whispered to herself, half exhilarated and half horrified by the sudden surging of her pulse. In a moment of clarity, all the texts she'd studied so diligently for her exams, the endless pages of Shakespeare and the Brontës, were more than just words on paper. Each one made perfect sense.

"Would you like to dance?" Mark had asked, crossing the room and holding out his hand to her. "I'd be honoured if you would."

She'd nodded, the words unable to form in her tight throat, and as he'd taken her hand in his strong warm one, Grace had felt such a jolt of energy that she'd gasped. Glancing up at Mark, she'd seen her own surprise echoed in his green eyes.

"Don't ever let go," he'd whispered, lacing his fingers through hers.

And Grace hadn't. They'd stayed together all that evening, dancing and talking and holding hands. When there'd been a break in the dancing and Mark had led her outside, Grace had known that he was going to kiss her and she'd thought her heart would burst with the perfection of it all. It was a beautiful night with a fat harvest moon sailing high in a sky the exact colour of the ink she'd written her exam answers in; Venus had shone brightly too as she'd hurried to catch the moon. Mark had drawn Grace close, his hands threading through her hair, and he'd stared down at her with wonder.

"You are so beautiful," he'd murmured. "You always were and you always will be."

And then he'd kissed her, the softest and most blissful kiss imaginable, and Grace's heart had melted. She'd known then that she adored him – and when Mark had told her he loved her, she hadn't doubted it for a second.

She loved him too and she always had.

From that night on they were inseparable. Of course, back then there were certain conventions and expectations, and Grace always respected her grandmother's rules. Nevertheless, every moment that Mark had free they spent together, and each was more magical than the last. Whenever she looked back on that time it seemed to Grace that the sun had shone incessantly and the colours had been brighter and more vivid than usual.

The first time they'd made love would be forever imprinted in her memory: the blue sky, the roughness of the picnic blanket against her skin, the tickling from a blade of grass, the calling buzzards, Mark's green eyes holding hers as he asked if she was all right…

All right? Grace was more than all right. Afterwards, she was walking on air and her nerves were crackling like space dust. She couldn't eat, she couldn't sleep and her every thought was filled with Mark. She'd never known it was possible to feel this way.

She'd spent her days giddy with happiness and her nights lying awake in bed, replaying the time they'd spent together and counting the hours until the sun rose and she could see him again. Her world had turned upside down; she was Juliet and Cathy and Héloïse all at once, and such happiness was almost unbearable. If it ended now she knew she would die.

Even all these years on, Grace could still feel the strength of those emotions. The feelings had never left her, it now appeared, but had merely been lying dormant. Of course she hadn't died when that magical summer had come to an end – but for a while it had really felt as though she might. The ache in her soul had been a physical pain. Time had done its thing and she'd moved on, got over it perhaps, but there was still a little piece of her heart that would be forever Mark Tuckett's. As she knocked on the farmhouse door now, she felt herself slip back into being the young and hopeful girl she'd once been.

"Can't you use the back door? You know we don't use the—"

It was Mark. It was really him and to Grace he didn't look so different. The thick dark curls were still a little longer than was conventional; admittedly they were sprinkled with silver now and he was deeply tanned, but that was all. He was wearing a waxed jacket, jeans and fisherman's socks, but beneath all this she knew he was as delicious as he'd always been.

For a second she couldn't speak. It was as though she'd only seen him yesterday, and she had the overwhelming sensation that she was coming to rest in a harbour after years of crossing wild and dangerous seas. His eyes were still the same intense shade of green, and the hands that had once made her quiver with longing looked just as strong and sensitive – surgeon's hands now. Grace knew, too, that if Mark were to fold her in his arms he would even smell the same. And his mouth? Would that feel the same on hers? She was shocked to discover just how much she longed to know the answer to this question.

As she held Jack tightly and fought to regain the power of speech, Grace wondered how she'd ever managed to be without Mark Tuckett for so long. Her every fibre wanted nothing more than to be held in his arms once again.

Mark was staring at her. It was impossible to tell what he was feeling. It could be shock or horror or, even worse, indifference. Not that it mattered a jot what he felt about her. She was here because of dear Isolde and the past was totally irrelevant. All that mattered was taking care of her friend. She must focus.

"Thank God you're here, Mark! You've got to come to Hallows now! My friend's been taken ill and I don't know what to do! I really need your help."

She gasped the words out without even thinking and Mark continued staring at her for a moment.

"Please!" Grace added. "I know I'm not your favourite person but Isolde's really sick and I need a doctor."

"Of course I'll come. Let me grab my bag and the car keys," Mark said. His voice was still as warm and rich as hot chocolate, but now it had an Antipodean lilt, a reminder of an entire life lived away from her.

Grace waited on the step, holding Jack close, until Mark reappeared with a doctor's bag and a set of car keys.

"Habit," he said seeing her glance at the bag. "I never go anywhere without this – and just as well, it seems. Hop into the Defender. It's bloody uncomfortable but Rob's taken the Jeep."

He strode towards the car and Grace followed, feeling dazed. Once in the Land Rover, which felt just like the one John had owned all those years ago, she watched him drive, the muscles of his thigh swelling beneath the fabric of his jeans. If it wasn't for Jack, a few wrinkles and the snow, they could have been driving to St Austell for an evening at the pictures. Grace's heart skittered at the memory like a pebble over a pond. They never did see much of any film they chose…

"What's happened to your friend?" Mark asked. He was looking straight ahead, his eyes fixed on the snowy lane, while Grace fought an illogical disappointment that he hadn't reached for her hand in the way he always used to.

"She fell earlier and she was out in the snow for a while. I don't think it was for long and she seemed all right until about ten minutes ago. She's usually fit and well, but she's in her late sixties and I'm worried about her."

"If you tell me the symptoms now, then it might help," Mark said curtly. Medic mode. Fine.

"She says she feels dizzy, her vision's blurred and she's cold – although that's hardly surprising with this weather," Grace told him. "Could it be a head injury?"

"Maybe. I'll know more when I've seen her. If it is, I'll drive her to the hospital. The electricity's out down here and will be for a while – and the roads aren't great, so an ambulance won't make it."

As he said this, the car hit a pothole with such violence that Grace's teeth rattled.

"Don't worry, I'll get my son to bring the Jeep back," Mark added, seeing the expression on her face. "I've driven this beast through the snow once already today and without any heating in the car we'd all freeze to death before we arrived. I've called him already but he isn't answering. Goodness knows where he is."

"He's with my niece, Poppy. They were helping the young man who's booked to stay in your holiday cottage. I think your son's quite taken with her," Grace told him.

"It happens," was all Mark said in reply, and they were pulling up at Hallows before Grace could pluck up the courage to ask what this was supposed to mean.

Isolde was still on the couch by the fire with her foot propped up, and Grace was relieved to see her friend glance up when they entered the room.

"I feel dreadful for causing such a fuss," Isolde said, looking tearful. "I'm ruining your Christmas Eve."

"Not at all," Mark assured her, crouching down and taking Isolde's wrist in his hand. "It's much cosier here than at my dad's place and I was only sitting around brooding. You've done me a favour."

"Are you sure? I feel so guilty for fetching you all the way over here."

Was it Grace's imagination or did Isolde look quite smug as she said this? As Mark slipped the blood-pressure cuff onto her arm she was perking up considerably. His bedside manner was doing the trick, Grace decided, and she was impressed with the gentle yet thorough way he was going about the examination. He'd followed his dreams and they'd evidently paid off a million times over. She hoped the same was true of her own life choices.

While Mark checked her friend, Grace popped Jack into his bouncy chair, which she'd placed as close to the wood burner as she dared, and went to make some tea. A few minutes later, Mark joined her in the kitchen. She didn't even need to turn around to know he was there; everything in her called out to him.

"Do you have any crisps?"

Grace sloshed hot water into mugs. "Hungry? There are mince pies if you are."

"I'm fine. The crisps are for Mrs Harper. She's got very low blood pressure and something salty will help raise it. That's why she's feeling a bit dizzy and clammy. She'll need water too, for hydration, and some sugary drinks as well if you can. Ribena's good, if you happen to have some."

Grace turned around, surprised. "Low blood pressure? Are you sure?"

Mark nodded. "It could be from the shock of falling or it could be something she's had for a while, but I promise you she isn't concussed. I've checked your friend carefully and she'll be fine. If I was in any doubt at all I'd drive her to hospital right now. The ankle's more of a worry. Do you have any ice?"

"Not in my fridge but…"

Grace raised a shoulder in the direction of the window and Mark laughed.

"Doh! If you give me a carrier bag I'll see what I can do about a makeshift ice pack; the water butt should have some on it, I'd have thought. I'll let you find some crisps. Raisins too, if you have any, and lots of fluids."

Mark went in search of ice and Grace tipped some Kettle Chips into a bowl and dug out the nuts and raisins from her supply of nibbles. Loading up a tray with snacks and tea, she rejoined her friend in the sitting room. Isolde was lying on the couch with her feet elevated, but when she caught sight of Grace she pushed herself up onto one elbow.

"What did he say? Has he changed? Is he still the one?"

Grace's mouth fell open. "Isolde Harper! Have you been having me on? Is this all an attempt to play cupid? Is this why you *forgot* to tell me John was in hospital?"

Was her mind playing tricks, or did her friend look a bit shifty? For a moment Grace felt quite cross – after all, she had been extremely worried about her friend – but then she remembered that Isolde really did have low blood pressure and had suffered quite a shock too.

"I genuinely didn't feel too well," Isolde was saying through a big mouthful of salty crisps, "but I'm feeling much better now. Sometimes these things happen for a reason. So, what was it like to see him again?"

Grace was about to say it felt a bit like being punched in the stomach, when Mark returned with a carrier bag filled with ice. He busied himself arranging it on Isolde's ankle and then took her blood pressure again.

"Much better," he announced. "Your colour's coming back too. I think I can be on my way now."

"No!" Isolde said quickly. "Not yet! I hate to be a demanding patient but I'm still feeling very wobbly. I'd feel much happier if you stayed here for an hour or so while I rested. You two could catch up in the kitchen while I sleep in here."

"Ever feel like you've been had?" Mark asked Grace when they settled down in the kitchen.

"I apologise," she said, blushing. "Isolde means well and she's a diehard romantic. I think she saw an opportunity to channel her inner cupid. She forgets we're nearly sixty."

"The joys of getting older, eh?" Mark said ruefully. "Rob keeps telling me I need to slow down."

She smiled. "You look just the same to me."

His green eyes held hers. "And you to me, Grace."

It was toasty warm with the Aga going but his words made her shiver. The candles wedged in bottles that she'd placed on the windowsills and dresser threw a warm and flattering light, so at least he couldn't see the full horror of her wrinkles, Grace thought. Then again, what did it matter if he did see them? They were no longer teenagers in love, even if she felt exactly the same about him as she'd always done. His greying hair, smile lines and extra weight didn't make the slightest bit of difference.

Her heart skipped a beat. Did this mean that she still loved him?

Knowing that he'd always been able to read her mind, Grace began to busy herself with more tea and more food – but he reached out and caught her wrist.

"Relax, Grace. This is strange for me too."

She sat down opposite him. "The thing is that it doesn't feel strange at all."

"No, you're right, it doesn't. You've not changed in the slightest."

She laughed and shook her head. "Oh, Mark! What nonsense! I'm old and grey and I weigh at least three stone more!"

"You still look absolutely beautiful to me," he said softly.

She waited for the laugh or the quip about needing glasses now, which would surely clarify this remark, but it didn't come. Instead, Mark reached out and took her hand again. The thrill that ignited in her blood when his fingers laced with hers in that old familiar way was undeniable.

And yes. She could see that he felt it too.

"It's so good to see you again," Mark said. The candlelight danced across his face, over those high cheekbones and full lips, and Grace knew instantly why there had never been anyone else for her. How could there possibly have been when she'd never stopped loving him, even though a whole lifetime had passed?

"It's good to see you too," she whispered.

His thumb traced a circle on her palm and her mouth dried. Her body remembered his touch. Her mind remembered everything. Most of all, her heart remembered how she'd always felt about him.

They talked then, their hands still linked and their conversation filling in the years. Stories. Adventures. Achievements. Careers. Success. Family. Sadness. On and on. The words came in a torrent while their tea cooled, the logs shifted in the firebox and Isolde pretended to sleep on the sofa. Resentments held for decades evaporated in the light of maturity and understanding as the adults they now were looked back with sympathy and fondness on the people they used to be. They'd been younger than Poppy and Rob were now, Grace pointed out with a laugh, half disbelieving and half despairing. They'd been little more than children. What chance had they really stood?

"We've wasted so much time," Mark said finally. "When you're young you think you've got forever and everything's so black and white. Somebody breaks your heart and that's it. Over, finished. You don't think to try and see things from their point of view. I wish I could go back in time and find that angry young man. I'd give him a few words of advice."

She looked at him across the table. "Ah, but would he listen any more than that headstrong young woman who was determined to follow her path too? No regrets, Mark. The choices we made then have made us who we are today."

"I'm a man sitting at a table, half a world away from his everyday life and holding hands with the woman I've always loved," Mark said quietly. "It might sound crazy but I have the strongest conviction that this is where I'm meant to be tonight. All I've ever done and all I've ever been have led me here and back to you."

And then Grace understood too how everything in her life had brought her to this moment. No half measures in friendship, career or love. Her whole life had been about taking the journey that would bring her to this exact point. It had been planned like an intricate tapestry, and it was only by standing back and looking carefully that she could see the full design. A design that had been there from the very start.

She squeezed his fingers. They were older now. The flames of youth had settled down to a warm glow, but the heat would be retained for a very long time if their love was tended properly. There were questions and logistics and a million other reasons why she should walk away, but Grace knew that this time she wouldn't be doing that.

"Can we start again?" Mark asked quietly, and Grace nodded.

"I'd like that. I'd like it very much indeed."

And when he kissed her, the soft touch of his mouth sending her tumbling back in time, so that she was restored as the girl she'd once been, Grace knew for certain that there had never been any half measures when it came to giving her heart.

This was her second chance for love and, true to that long-ago promise to her grandmother, Grace knew she would give it everything.

Epilogue

Christmas Day

Christmas morning dawned cold and bright, the low winter sunshine turning the world into a perfect replica of the beautifully iced cake that took pride of place on the kitchen table at Hallows. The similarity had soon ended though: unlike the cake's unblemished icing, the snowy world outside was now peppered with footprints and pockmarked where gloved hands had scooped out snowballs from drifts or the tops of walls. On the lawn sat a wonky snowman, with a rather bemused expression thanks to Jack having placed his eyes and nose with creativity rather than accuracy. Meanwhile, a violent snowball battle was taking place between Nick and Rob, with Poppy acting as referee.

While Nick pelted Rob and Poppy yelled encouragement, Grace was preparing what was turning out to be the oddest Christmas dinner ever: a mishmash of the bits and pieces she'd brought from London and what Nick and Rob had rescued from Isolde's freezer. Although the electricity supply had been restored to their small hamlet just before midnight, it had been far too late to prevent the contents defrosting, so the boys had been dispatched to salvage whatever they could. They'd come back laden with pizzas, chicken nuggets, sausage rolls, Chinese food and three Arctic Rolls. It was hardly festive fare, but once it was all presented alongside the turkey and trimmings Grace thought it would be fine – if unusual.

"Three Arctic Rolls?" she'd asked Isolde, who'd grimaced.

"Alan loved them but I can't bear the things. Honestly, Arctic Roll is the one thing I don't miss! Feel free to bin those."

"No way!" Mark had scooped the packets up in a flash. "I love these! Takes me right back to being a kid! They were a treat at our place. Just ask the old man. In fact, I might even bring him one at visiting time."

Grace had laughed. "I should imagine they're a bit far gone to make it all the way to Truro! Give them to me. Maybe I can scrape them out of the packaging and improvise with a trifle. I don't think it's a good idea to refreeze them if they've gone soft."

She did rustle up a trifle too, although it was a rather strange affair, but for once preparing food for her guests wasn't Grace's main concern; she was far more excited about the people she would be eating it with. Or, rather, *the person*. Mark. Her Mark. Here and real and as wonderful now as he'd been all those years ago. She could hardly bear to let him out of her sight, unable to shake off the fear that this was all a dream and that she would wake up very soon.

To make certain, she pinched herself. Ouch! No, she was most definitely awake, which meant that this was undoubtedly real and the most magical Christmas ever. It didn't even matter that Grace hadn't slept because she and Mark had stayed up all night talking. She didn't feel at all tired! In fact, she was brimming with energy. They had so much catching up to do, so many plans to make and just not enough hours to fit it all in. Having missed all these years, neither of them intended to waste another moment of their second chance. Quite what they would do was still hazy but, whatever happened next, Grace knew it was going to be a huge adventure.

Rob had been thrilled and not at all upset to see his father holding Grace's hand. He'd been so wrapped up in Poppy that it had taken him a while to notice, but when he had he'd just said that it was *cool*.

"Cool?" Mark had echoed. "You don't mind? It's OK with you?"

"Course it is," Rob had said. "Jeez, Dad, it's not as though you and Ma are still married. Anyway, she's got Neal."

"I've no idea who Neal is," Mark had replied, "but I'll take it that's a good thing and you approve."

"Neal's a knob," Rob had told him cheerfully, "but Mum likes him and she's happy, which is the main thing. And now you're happy too. That's awesome. Em will be rapt too."

So they had the blessing of Mark's children. That meant a lot.

As though sensing these thoughts, Mark wrapped his arms around her and dropped a kiss onto the top of her head.

"What are you thinking about?"

"You," Grace said, rising onto her tiptoes to kiss him and still unable to believe that this was really happening. "Us."

"Us." Mark shook his head in incredulity. "I still can't believe there's an 'us'. It feels like a dream, a wonderful one, but still a dream. If Isolde hadn't tripped and if Dad hadn't fallen, then who knows?" A shadow flittered across his face as he thought about John still in the hospital. "Not that either of those things are good, but without them we might never have bumped into one another again."

"Perhaps something good can come out of what seems like something bad? Maybe we can take comfort in that?"

"Maybe," Mark agreed thoughtfully. "Rob's certainly keen to stay and help, and he seems very excited about the farm. He's already discussed it with Dad, apparently, and it seems I'm the last to know what they've been planning. The old man must be on the mend."

"He seemed fine when you spoke to him earlier, didn't he?"

"He was his usual grumpy self. Wanted to know how the hell I had time to be on the telephone when I should have been tending the farm," Mark said with a resigned smile. "When I told him Rob was in charge, he seemed more than happy. He doesn't trust me with the place but it seems he does trust his grandson, which is just as well. Rob seems to fit right in. I mean, look at him now! You'd never know he's spent most of his life in one-hundred-degree heat!"

Out in the garden the chilly air rang with laughter as Nick and Rob pelted each other with more snowballs while Poppy and Jack watched.

"It's worked out beautifully," said Grace in wonder.

"Like it's meant to be?"

"Exactly that. The timings. The people who've come together. The snowfall that trapped us all here for just the right amount of time. It feels as though it was meant to happen." Grace knew this sounded fanciful, but to her it seemed that something very magical had taken place this Christmas. "Does that sound daft to you?"

Mark smiled. "I'm not too old to believe in magic and wishes coming true. I don't think I've ever seen Rob smile so much either. Not since we last won the Ashes, anyway!"

Rob and Poppy had returned last night hand in hand and bubbling with excitement, full of plans for their future. Rob was adamant he wanted to remain in Cornwall and take over the running of Tucketts' Farm, but when he looked at Poppy with such tenderness and love in those familiar green eyes, Grace knew it wasn't just the farm he was staying for.

"They look so happy," she said.

Mark kissed her. "They're not the only ones."

"All right, you two lovebirds, give it a rest or I might start to feel ill again!" Isolde limped into the kitchen, leaning heavily on the elaborately carved walking cane that Mark had unearthed from under the stairs at Tucketts' Farm. "Grace, could you let him go just long enough to pour me some mulled wine?"

"Why don't you two go and relax in the sitting room? I've got this," said Mark, wielding the ladle. "I can handle the dinner too."

The Aga was crammed to maximum capacity and the kitchen was filled with delicious aromas. Chestnut stuffing, pepperoni pizza, roast potatoes, chow mein and turkey jostled for pole position with bread sauce, plum pudding and mulled wine.

"Are you sure?" Grace asked.

In answer he flicked her with a tea towel. "I can perform a heart bypass, so I think I'll just about cope. Go on, have a break."

Now that the electricity had returned, the sitting room was at its festive best. The tree twinkled, the scent of pine filled the air and the wood burner crackled. Beside it, Isolde's spaniels slumbered with their heads on their paws and their noses twitching with doggy dreams. Isolde was settled on the sofa with her foot up on a stool and Grace sat beside her, passing the mulled wine across.

"Alan would have liked him." Isolde inclined her head in the direction of the kitchen, and Grace knew this was the highest praise indeed.

They sat quietly for a moment watching the dancing flames, both deep in thought.

"I miss Alan," Isolde said quietly.

"I know you do. I can't even begin to imagine how much."

"And I wouldn't ever want you to. Life is about living and seizing every moment," Isolde told her. "It's also about new directions and adventures. I'm looking forward to teaching Nick the things that Alan taught me over the years. It feels as though I'm keeping part of him alive by passing his knowledge on to someone who'll appreciate it. Does that make sense? It feels like Alan's got another chance to show just how talented he was and to teach photography again."

Grace did see. "It makes perfect sense. I think it's a wonderful idea."

"It will keep my Lizzie quiet too," Isolde said with a sigh of relief. "She'll be glad I'm not on my own – and that's one thing less for her to fret about."

Grace was pleased too. It was already clear that Nick York was a kind young man with a big heart, and it seemed that both he and her dear friend would find peace and healing in the months ahead. What Nick's story would be, only time would tell – but where better to find out than up here on the Cornish moors? It was a wonderful place to take stock and find your path.

Where she would go next was still unknown too, but this sense of nebulousness filled Grace with excitement. The time to step back from the pressures of her job was drawing close and, after that, who knew? One thing she was certain of was that there would be travel involved and a trip to Australia. Warm climates, new places and friends as yet unmade lay in wait. The future would unfold at its own pace and she was content with this idea. It was the way things were, the way they should be, and it had taken her over fifty years to understand this.

A rush of cool air and a sudden rise in noise levels announced that the snowballers had come in to dry out. Before long, Hallows was filled with chatter and excitement. The last-minute arrival of her brother Ned and his wife Amy, both missing Jack and Poppy far too much to bear staying away on Christmas Day, was greeted with cries of joy from their grandson, who waved his chubby starfish hands in delight.

Leaving Isolde in the peace of the sitting room, Grace joined the others in the kitchen, where hugs and kisses and mulled wine were in abundance. As she heard Ned apologise to Poppy and tell her gruffly that he was proud of her and loved her, tears sprang to Grace's eyes – and when Poppy threw her arms around him and said she loved him too, Grace had to step into the hallway to recover herself. She didn't have long to do this because Mark, in spite of his heart-bypassing skills, was soon calling for her to judge whether the turkey was done. Simultaneously, Ned was demanding that she opened the most expensive wine from their grandparents' cellar. With a smile, Grace dabbed her eyes on her sleeve and stepped back into the chaos of Christmas with her loved ones, old and new.

Some hours later, once the food was eaten, her guests had either slumped in front of the fire or returned home. Jack was asleep in his cot and Poppy and Rob were curled up on the sofa watching a film.

Grace and Mark had managed to visit John Tuckett earlier, who'd been unsurprised to see them together; in his usual blunt way he'd wondered what had taken them so long. Now that the day was done and everyone seemed content, the two of them wandered out into the snowy landscape. Enfolded in one another's arms, they stared up at the star-sprinkled sky. The world was still and sparkling and filled with possibilities that only a day ago would have seemed more like impossibilities. *Peace and goodwill to all men*, thought Grace, *and love and happiness too.* After all, wasn't this what Christmas was all about? Love, just like Christmas and anything worth having, didn't come in half measures. You gave it everything you had and a little more besides.

Above them, the clouds began to thicken, the stars tucked themselves away and the snow started to fall again. Meanwhile the windows of Hallows shone with warm light, woodsmoke spiralled up into the sky and love wrapped itself around Grace's heart – a second-chance love that she knew was the greatest gift of all.

Hand in hand, Grace and Mark walked back to Hallows while the snow fell softly, dusting out their footprints, erasing any tracks left by wildlife and making the whole world perfect and new again.

THE END

Sign up for Ruth's Newsletter to find out about future books as soon as they're released!

I really hope you have enjoyed reading THE SEASON FOR SECOND CHANCES. If you did I would really appreciate a review on Amazon. It makes all the difference for a writer.

Amazon UK

Amazon.com

You might also enjoy my other books:

Runaway Summer: Polwenna Bay 1

A Time for Living: Polwenna Bay 2

Winter Wishes: Polwenna Bay 3

Treasure of the Heart: Polwenna Bay 4

Recipe for Love: Polwenna Bay 5

Magic in the Mist: Polwenna Bay novella

Cornwall for Christmas: Polwenna Bay novella

The Island Legacy

Escape for the Summer

Escape for Christmas

Hobb's Cottage

Weight till Christmas

The Wedding Countdown

Dead Romantic

Katy Carter Wants a Hero

Katy Carter Keeps a Secret

Ellie Andrews Has Second Thoughts

Amber Scott is Starting Over

Writing as Jessica Fox

The One That Got Away

Eastern Promise

Hard to Get

Unlucky in Love

Always the Bride

Writing as Holly Cavendish

Looking for Fireworks

Writing as Georgie Carter

The Perfect Christmas

ABOUT THE AUTHOR

Ruth Saberton is the bestselling author of *Katy Carter Wants a Hero* and *Escape for the Summer*. She also writes upmarket commercial fiction under the pen names Jessica Fox, Georgie Carter and Holly Cavendish.

Born in London, Ruth now lives in beautiful Cornwall. She has travelled to many places and recently returned from living in the Caribbean but nothing compares to the rugged beauty of the Cornish coast. Ruth loves to chat with readers so please visit her Facebook Author page and follow her on Twitter.

Twitter: @ruthsaberton
Facebook: Ruth Saberton
www.ruthsaberton.com

Printed in Great Britain
by Amazon